This book is to be returned on or before
the last date stamped below.

Please return on or before the latest date above.
You can renew online at *www.kent.gov.uk/libs*
or by telephone 08458 247 200

CUSTOMER SERVICE EXCELLENCE

Libraries & Archives

00884\DTP\RN\07.07   LIB 7

Maggie's gaze flicked to the pregnancy test he was holding. She saw a pretty pink plus sign and was too stunned to speak.

Pregnant. Pregnant. *A baby. A baby. A baby.* Her hands shook. But how? It couldn't be. It had to be wrong.

'It's positive,' she said, looking at him for confirmation.

'I can see that,' he said grimly.

Maggie could hear him speaking, but none of his words made sense. Didn't he remember she was infertile? 'No. I mean.... I can't...I'm not supposed to be able to fall pregnant.'

Wrapping her head around this was taking some time. And despite it all her insides were singing. *Yes, singing.*

A baby. A baby. A baby.

Amy Andrews has always loved writing, and still can't quite believe that she gets to do it for a living. Creating wonderful heroines and gorgeous heroes and telling their stories is an amazing way to pass the day. Sometimes they don't always act as she'd like them to—but then neither do her kids, so she's kind of used to it. Amy lives in the very beautiful Samford Valley, with her husband and aforementioned children, along with six brown chooks and two black dogs. She loves to hear from her readers. Drop her a line at www.amyandrews.com.au

Recent titles by the same author:

THE BILLIONAIRE CLAIMS HIS WIFE**
GREEK DOCTOR, CINDERELLA BRIDE
THE SINGLE DAD'S NEW-YEAR BRIDE*
DR ROMANO'S CHRISTMAS BABY*

Brisbane General Hospital
**Short story for *Australian Billionaires* anthology

A DOCTOR,
A NURSE:
A CHRISTMAS
BABY

BY
AMY ANDREWS

All the characters in this book have no existence outside
the imagination of the author, and have no relation
whatsoever to anyone bearing the same name or names.
They are not even distantly inspired by any individual
known or unknown to the author, and all the incidents
are pure invention.

First published in Great Britain 2009
Large Print edition 2010
Harlequin Mills & Boon Limited,
Eton House, 18-24 Paradise Road,
Richmond, Surrey TW9 1SR

© Amy Andrews 2009

ISBN: 978 0 263 21086 6

Harlequin Mills & Boon policy is to use papers that are
natural, renewable and recyclable products and made
from wood grown in sustainable forests. The logging and
manufacturing process conform to the legal environmental
regulations of the country of origin.

Printed and bound in Great Britain
by CPI Antony Rowe, Chippenham, Wiltshire

A DOCTOR,
A NURSE:
A CHRISTMAS
BABY

This book is dedicated
to the Radio Lollipop volunteers at the
Royal Children's Hospital in Brisbane.
You bring music and distraction
into a sterile, scary world.
Thank you.

CHAPTER ONE

MAGGIE GREEN WISHED the universe had given her some inkling that October morning as she descended the stairs two at a time to the squealing of the emergency pager that it was going to tilt on its axis. Instead, as the shrill tone echoed around the cement labyrinth of the hospital fire escape, it appeared to be just another day, just another code blue at the Brisbane Children's Hospital.

She had no way of suspecting, as she rushed headlong into the emergency department resus bay, the total and utter cataclysmic effect of one Dr Nash Reece. Oh, sure, she'd heard about him. Who hadn't? The grapevine had been running hot over the country-boy charmer and every female from the cleaning staff through to the director of nursing were swooning over his sexy strut.

But she wasn't a swooner. And things like love or lust at first sight were for teenagers. And she was a good two decades past that. Or so she'd thought.

Nash glanced up from the mottled, struggling, unconscious infant at the nurse who'd just arrived on the scene. She was slightly puffed, her generous chest heaving in and out beneath the navy of her polo shirt. Despite her breathlessness there was a calm confidence about her and he smiled.

'Good. You're just in time. I'm pretty sure she's going to need intubation.'

He shifted his focus back to his patient. The drugs they'd given to stop her tiny body seizing were playing havoc with her respiratory drive and she wasn't breathing nearly as well as he liked. He held an ambu-bag in situ over the little girl's face, supporting her weak respiratory effort.

Maggie stared at the bluest eyes she'd ever seen. Even downcast they were quite spectacular. Combined with a killer jaw line dusted in stubble and wavy dark blond hair pushed back off his tanned forehead and lapping over his collar in true cowboy fashion, she really did swoon. A little.

Oblivious to the rush around her, the controlled chaos, the trilling of alarms and the sobbing of a distraught woman, Maggie's stomach did a three-sixty-degree flop.

Nash looked up amused to see the nurse hadn't moved. He felt his lips tugging upwards despite the gravity of the situation. He knew that look. Women had looked at him like that for as long as he could remember. But it was the surprise on her face that was most intriguing. 'You are the ICU nurse?'

Maggie nodded absently, feeling totally disconnected from her brain as that slow, lazy, cocky smile hit its mark. She couldn't ever remember being rendered mute by the sheer presence of a man.

'Well I think you might need to come closer,

Sister. I'm gonna need a hand and I don't think you're going to be able to reach from there.'

Maggie blinked, the use of her nursing title cutting through the daze. Right. She was the ICU nurse. That's why she was here. She was responsible for the airway. It was her job. Still, his rich voice oozed over her like warm mud from hot springs and for one crazy moment she wanted to dive in head first and wallow.

Finally her brain kicked in and her legs moved. She took two strides and was at the head of the open cot, staring straight into Nash Reece's blue, blue gaze.

Nash smiled. She'd looked good from a distance. She looked better up close. 'Where's your reg?' he asked.

'He's seeing a ward patient over the other side of the hospital.'

Her voice was breathy and she hated it. For God's sake, she had to be a good decade older than him. She wasn't remotely interested. And even if she was, why would he be interested in her? A forty-year-old divorcee who hadn't been in a relationship for so long she'd forgotten what was required?

If his rep was anything to go by, she was way out of his league. She was way past nightclubs and partying. She came to work, she volunteered at Radio Giggle, she tended her garden, read voraciously and she slept.

Oh, God—she was turning into a hermit. A cradle-snatching hermit. All she needed was a couple of cats and she'd be the full catastrophe. She cleared her throat. 'He'll be here soon.'

She looked a little het up and he couldn't help stirring a little. 'You okay to do this?'

Maggie wanted to bristle. She wanted to say, Listen sonny, I was helping with intubations while you were till wearing baggy pants. But she didn't. She just nodded and asked, 'What size?'

He sent her another slow, lazy smile. 'Four.'

Maggie lowered her gaze, feeling uncharacteristically flustered. She'd been in hundreds of medical emergencies and had never been anything other than ruthlessly efficient. This time would be no different.

She turned to the resus trolley she knew would be behind her, reached inside the drawer and pulled out the requested endotracheal tube. She opened the packaging and squirted some lubricant on the end of the narrow curved tube.

The tone on the sats monitor started to dip and the infant's heart rate started to drop. Instantly they were both alert, the funny zing between them forgotten.

'Heart rate falling,' Maggie said her gaze flicking to the green squiggle behind Nash's head. 'One hundred.'

They watched the infant's chest as her respiratory rate dropped off further. 'Sats ninety-two,' Maggie relayed, watching the blue number on the LCD screen dip lower and lower.

'Okay, no time to wait for the ICU reg. Let's do it.'

Maggie couldn't agree more. Normally working with a doctor—*a registrar*—she didn't know made her nervous as hell in these fraught situations. But strangely she wasn't. She didn't know Nash from a bar of soap—apart from his lady-killer rep—but his supreme confidence was utterly assuring.

'Let's give her some vecuronium, Zoe,' Nash said to one of the emergency nurses as he pulled down on the infant's chin, opening her mouth for a brief inspection before placing the mask firmly back in place. 'Have we got some atropine drawn up?'

Maggie blinked as the man with the slow, sexy smile vanished and morphed into a consummate professional. She followed suit, ignoring the fierce jolt of sexual attraction and becoming the experienced PICU nurse, calm and in control.

'Vecuronium on board,' Zoe said as she pushed the drug into the child's drip. 'Atropine ready if you need it.'

Nash nodded and started taking over the infant's breathing altogether as the drug acted quickly, paralysing all muscle function. 'Okay,'

he murmured giving some big breaths to pre-
oxygenate. The sats came up to one hundred per
cent and the heart rate rocketed into the one
hundred and sixties.

'Right,' he said, dropping the bag. 'Let's go.'

Maggie passed him the laryngoscope and
everyone held their breath as he expertly slipped
the metal into the child's mouth. The light at the
end allowed Nash to visualise the tiny white
vocal cords.

'Tube.'

He held out his hand as the other one applied
pressure through the handle of the scope to keep
the patient's jaw open. He was like a surgeon
asking for an instrument, his eyes never leaving
the target.

Maggie passed it to him positioned correctly
so he could slip it down the blade of the laryngoscope and push it through the cords in one
fluid movement.

'Heart rate one fifty-nine. Sats ninety-eight,'
she said quietly.

Nash nodded as he angled the tube in. He'd been about to ask. His back was to the monitor so he couldn't see the figures. All he knew for sure was that while he was performing the intubation the patient wasn't getting any respiratory input at all. The drug she'd been given had stopped her breathing altogether and the longer he took, the more he deprived her body of vital oxygen.

'Cricoid pressure,' he murmured.

Maggie automatically reached for the child's neck using her thumb and forefinger to apply gentle pressure mid-trachea to the cricoid cartilage, temporarily occluding the oesophagus to prevent aspiration of stomach contents into the lungs.

Nash was impressed with the nurse's quick, sure location and technique. Often the pressure applied was too much, deviating the airway anatomy, but her technique was perfect.

'Heart rate one sixty-five. Sats ninety-two.'

Nash nodded as he completed the procedure. 'I'm in.'

He held the tube in place as Maggie attached

the bag and puffed in a couple of gentle breaths. The patient's tiny chest rose and fell. Rose and fell. Her sats climbed.

'Do you want to listen?' Maggie asked.

Nash nodded. He took the bag from her, keeping a firm grasp on the tube. He held very still as she carefully pulled his stethoscope from his neck, and placed it in his ears. Her gaze brushed his as she did so and then stuck. Her cheeks were a pretty pink and even though a part of his brain was listening for the whoosh of breath sounds as she moved the bell of the stethoscope around the patient's chest, the other part was noticing her deep brown eyes, her high cheekbones, her wide, full lips.

'What a beautiful noise,' he murmured, not taking his eyes off her.

Maggie swallowed. This close, he was incredibly handsome. His eye colour defied belief. A clear pale blue, like tropical waters or maybe, depending on his mood, glacial ice. His skin was tanned, stretched nicely across prominent cheekbones, and he had deep crinkles on his forehead and tiny lines around his eyes like he enjoyed a good laugh as much as he enjoyed a good dose of Australian sunshine.

She became aware she was staring again and snapped herself out of it. 'Should we get this tube taped in?' she prompted.

'Good idea,' Nash murmured.

Maggie dragged her gaze away, grateful to have a job that required looking down and not up. She'd applied the first piece of tape, ignoring his long tanned fingers holding the tube firmly in place, when the ICU reg finally made his entrance.

'Mac,' Nash greeted him. 'You're a little too late.'

'Sorry,' Mac Caldwell panted, bending over and clutching his side. 'I ran all the way.'

Nash laughed. 'Have a seat, man. Crisis over.'

Maggie found concentrating on the finicky task of wrapping zinc tape around the tube even more difficult with him being so close. His chest was at her head level and his body heat combined with his intoxicating aftershave formed a potent mix.

Her downward gaze took in the rich tan of his chinos and the obvious flatness of his abdomen beneath the casual masculinity of his checked shirt. He wore it open at the neck and rolled up to his elbows revealing tanned forearms in stark contrast to the covering of blond hairs.

She listened as he filled Mac in on the case and spoke with just the right amounts of empathy, confidence and authority to the infant's distressed mother.

'Let's hook her up to the portable ventilator,' Nash requested as the last tape was secured around the tube. 'We'll get an X-ray to check the tube position, and can we load her with some anti-convulsants, please, Zoe?'

'I'll just let the consultant know we've got ourselves another customer,' Mac said, excusing himself to find a phone.

Maggie fussed with the tapes, trimming one end that had been stuck across the little girl's tiny ear, hyper-aware of Nash still standing close. Her elbow occasionally came into contact with his shirt and she seemed to be tuned into his every move, every breath.

'Thank you…' Nash looked at the nametag clipped to his assistant's collar. She had a smiley-face sticker over her picture and a red heart sticker covering her surname. 'Maggie. Thank you, Maggie.'

Her hands stilled as his voice washed over her like warm treacle.

She chanced a look at him and immediately wished she hadn't. He was smiling one of those *hey-baby* smiles and she was equal parts turned on and annoyed. Annoyed won out.

Some men were just too charming for their own good. Some men just didn't know how to turn it off. She aimed for nonchalance with her shrug. 'Just doing my job.'

'Ah, but you do it so well.'

Maggie felt things shift inside at the suggestive quality of his low, sexy voice. She sniffed, not at all comfortable with shifting innards. This man was too young and too sure of himself by far. 'Well, I would, wouldn't I? I have been doing this for a very long time.'

Nash chuckled at the emphasis. He got it—she didn't approve of him flirting with someone of her years. 'I love experienced women.'

Maggie refused to be flattered by such a consummate flirt. She raised an eyebrow. 'Only experienced women?'

He grinned. 'Okay, you got me.'

'Nash?'

He looked away from Maggie reluctantly. 'Yes, Zoe?'

'Can you assess the kid in cube two for me? I think he can progress to hourly nebs now.'

'Sure, be right there,' Nash said. He turned back to Maggie. 'I'll be seeing you around, Maggie.'

She sent him a stiff smile. *Not if she could help it.*

Maggie finally got to lunch at two o'clock. The day had been crazy-busy and everyone's lunch-breaks had been pushed back. She found an isolated table in the almost empty canteen, glad she didn't have to spend her thirty minutes making small talk with anyone. She cracked the lid on her calorie-laden fizzy drink and sank her teeth into the divine-smelling hot meat pie.

A pair of freakish blue eyes rose unbidden and she shook her head to dispel them from her mind. There'd been no time this morning to think about her weird response to Nash Reece and she was damned if she was going to spend her precious break thinking about him either.

'Now that's a nice healthy lunch.'

And sometimes the universe was just out to get you.

Maggie tensed as the voice behind her took form and shape in front of her. Hunky, sexy form and shape.

'May I join you?'

Maggie looked around at the other empty tables. 'Plenty of places to sit,' she said pointedly.

Nash suppressed the urge to chuckle. He liked a woman who could hold her own with him. She reminded him of the females he'd grown up around. His five sisters, his mother, his cousins. Country women were no shrinking violets and although he'd spent his life perfecting how to twist them around his fingers, he admired the hell out of their spirit.

'Ah, but this is my favourite table.' Nash grinned and pulled up a chair.

'Gee. Lucky me.'

'We haven't formally met.' He stuck out his hand. 'Nash Reece.'

No way on earth was Maggie going to touch him. If he could unsettle her with his mere presence, God alone knew what would happen if she allowed her skin to come into contact with his. She took another bite of pie, feeling an instant revival to her flagging blood-sugar level. 'I know who you are.'

Nash chuckled at her deliberate snub. 'Ah, my reputation precedes me, I see.'

She looked at his totally unrepentant face. 'Try to look as if it upsets you,' she said derisively.

He grinned at her. She had the deepest brown

eyes he'd ever seen. They reminded him of his grandmother's double chocolate fudge brownies. And, man, he was suddenly ravenous for them.

'So…Maggie? Maggie who?'

She took a swig of her drink. 'Maggie from ICU.'

He quirked an eyebrow. Maggie from ICU was playing hard to get. Well, there was a first time for everything. 'So, Maggie from ICU, are you doing anything tonight? Do you fancy getting a bite to eat with me?'

Maggie almost inhaled her drink into her lungs his question startled her so completely. She coughed and spluttered so much that in a final humiliation Nash reached across and belted her between the shoulder blades a couple of times.

His hand moved to her shoulder and he grinned. 'You okay?'

Not remotely. She shrugged his hand away. 'Fine.'

He gave her a few moments before he asked again. 'Well?'

Was he serious? She looked at him—yep, he

was. It had been three years since she'd been on a date. And certainly a good decade since she'd been with anyone whose age fell in the thirties. 'No.'

'Tomorrow night?'

'No.'

Nash shrugged. 'Well I'm easy—'

'Clearly,' she interrupted.

Nash grinned and continued. 'I can fit in with you.'

Maggie shook her head, exasperated by his persistence. He had his elbows on the table, emphasising his wide shoulders. He was big and broad and loomed at her from the opposite side, taking up all the space. 'You don't like to take no for an answer, do you?'

'Why ignore what's going on between us, Maggie? I'm attracted to you.' He watched her pale and her wide brown eyes practically double in size. 'I'm pretty sure you're attracted to me. Why should we pretend otherwise?'

Maggie stared at him. *Was he insane?* He reminded her of a kid expecting instant gratification in that infantile egocentric way of theirs. But they weren't kids. They were grown-ups and adults were supposed to be a little more cautious. There were rules and etiquette.

'How old are you, Nash?'

Ah. 'I don't care about the age difference.'

'How old?' she insisted.

'Just turned the big three zero.'

Maggie nodded—just as she'd suspected. She wished for a brief second she was thirty again. But then reality invaded. She'd been a mess at thirty. She'd been dealing—very badly—with the heartbreak of her infertility and the ink had still been wet on her divorce papers. She was in a much better place now.

'And how old do you think I am?'

Nash looked directly at her. 'Twenty-six.'

Maggie burst out laughing. She had to give him his due, he hadn't batted an eyelid. She knew that she was looking pretty good for a forty-year-old woman but no one would ever mistake her for twenty-six. 'Does that line work with everyone?'

Nash laughed with her. 'Never had to use it before. No one's ever knocked me back.'

His eyes crinkled at the corners and it was very, very sexy. 'Oh, dear. Do you think your ego can stand it?'

'It's pretty robust.'

Maggie grinned despite herself. She did not want to be charmed by him but his easy charisma and self-deprecation made an irresistible combination. 'I'll just bet it is.'

He sat and watched her as she returned her attention to her lunch. Her teeth bit into the pastry of her pie and flakes stuck to her lips before her tongue darted out to remove them. It shouldn't be erotic—she was just eating, for crying out loud—but it was. God knew, he wanted to lick them away himself.

For his own sanity he moved his gaze upwards. Her short brown hair with chunky blonde streaks looked salon perfect. Her layered fringe swept across her forehead from a side parting. The rest of it fell in fashionably shaggy layers and feathered down her nape into fine wisps.

She finished her pie and patted her mouth with her serviette. If she hadn't seemed so totally oblivious to his reaction, he'd have suspected she was deliberately trying to provoke him. He certainly would have expected it from any other woman.

'Well?'

Maggie had tried to ignore him as she'd eaten but his intense blue gaze had made it impossible. She sighed. 'I'm forty, Nash.'

He shrugged. 'So?'

'So? So I'm a whole decade older than you.'

'So?'

'I was in high school when you were running around in nappies.'

'So?'

'I got married while you were still in primary school.'

Nash's gaze flicked to her left hand. No ring. No telltale white mark. 'So?'

'I've been divorced longer than you've been a doctor.'

He smiled at her. 'You're available, then?'

She shot him an impatient look. 'Nash don't you think you should be playing with women your own age?'

He reached across the table and picked up her hand. 'Maggie from ICU, you look better than any woman I've ever met.'

She could feel herself blushing beneath his intense gaze. She was drowning in the warmth of his tropical island gaze and her pulse hammered where his thumb drew slow circles at her wrist.

Damn it all—she would not be flattered by his easy words. She wasn't going to get involved with a man ten years her junior. Especially one who dated for sport and made her breathless with just one look. That would just be plain dumb. And she wasn't that hard up for company.

Maggie removed her hand. 'I'm going to do you a favour, Nash Reece. I'm going to turn you down. And you should be grateful. Men like you need a woman like me—'

'That's what I've been trying to tell you,' he interrupted.

She smiled. 'A woman who'll say no. Too many yes-women make Nash a spoilt boy. You'll thank me for it one day.'

He chuckled. 'I doubt it.'

She crunched up her paper bag and screwed the lid back on her empty drink bottle and then stood. 'Yeah well, your wife will.'

Nash really laughed then. He had no intention of ever marrying. And women had tried. Man, had they tried. Country girls, yearning for an escape from the outback had tried, city girls wanting to snare a doctor had tried. But he had a career plan carefully mapped out that did not involve weddings, and nothing was more important to him than that.

'Wife? Nope. Not me. Besides, I'm already married. To my career. I'm on a path.'

Maggie was surprised to see a suddenly serious

side to the flirty man who'd charmed himself into the seat opposite. He was once again the serious doctor from this morning. She wondered how many women got to see beneath the playboy exterior to the goal-driven man. 'And yet you have time to date?'

Nash grinned again. 'I do allow myself some diversions. Come on, Maggie. You know you want to.'

She shook her head, even though he was right. She did want to. It was crazy—but she did. Still, she knew enough about Nash Reece in a handful of minutes to know that one date would never be enough. 'Denial is good for the soul.'

'Denial sucks.'

He reminded her again of a child seeking instant gratification and she laughed. Yes. Yes it did. 'Goodbye, Dr Reece.'

Nash watched her turn away, the creamy skin of her neck exposed as she twisted, pulling her shirt across her chest. 'I'm gonna keep asking,' he called after her.

She stopped and looked back at him as his silky promise stroked insidiously along her pelvic floor. 'There's a shock.'

Nash chuckled. 'I'll be seeing you around, Maggie from ICU.'

They were the same words he'd used that morning and they had a preternatural foreboding to them. 'Don't count on it.'

He worked in A and E. She worked two floors up in ICU. As far as hospitals went they were totally different worlds. And after today she had no intention of letting him into hers. Ever.

CHAPTER TWO

THE NEXT DAY was her day off but Maggie found herself at the hospital anyway. She was actively involved in Radio Giggle and volunteered there regularly. In fact, she'd been on the original committee that had pushed for its establishment after seeing the success of Radio Lollipop during her stint at Great Ormond Street in London.

Maggie had seen their humble service expand over the years from a handful of people launching the first two-hour broadcast to a band of volunteers that worked tirelessly, promoting the healing power of play.

Radio Giggle volunteers actively engaged children throughout the hospital in a variety of entertainment, from helping with the shows, requesting songs and hearing themselves on the radio through to bedside crafts, games and other activities for those children unable to make it to the studio.

In fact, anything that could be done to help make a child's stay in hospital a little less frightening and a lot more fun, Radio Giggle were on it.

It wasn't her usual day to volunteer but Ross Calvin, Giggle's programme manager and only paid employee, was off sick today and had rung to ask her if she could take his place. Maggie hadn't hesitated. Not being able to have her own children had been a huge blow, but hanging out with these kids helped to fill the gap.

Five-year-old Douglas Werner, a long-term in-patient, was the first person she saw when she entered the Radio Giggle office.

'Dougy.' She smiled and crouched down accepting the little boy's enthusiastic cuddle.

'He's been asking for you.'

Maggie looked up to see fifteen-year-old Christine Leek, a cystic fibrosis patient and another regular in the Radio Giggle studio. 'Well, here I am,' she said, giving the little boy a quick rib tickle and laughing at his endearing shriek.

'Guess what?' Christine spoke over the top of Doug. 'Ross said I could conduct the interview today all by myself.' She looked over Maggie's shoulder. 'Have you seen him yet?'

Maggie watched while the painfully thin teenager shifted from foot to foot, her lip pulled between her bottom teeth. Christine was a blossoming DJ who wanted a career in community radio and spent every possible minute with the Radio Giggle organisation. 'I'm afraid Ross is off sick today.'

'Oh.'

Maggie couldn't bear to see her so crestfallen. 'You can still do it, though,' she reassured her. Christine's face lit up like a fireworks display and Maggie felt her heart contract.

'Really?' she squeaked.

'Of course.' Maggie laughed. 'You know your way around the dials better than I do.'

They went through to the brightly painted studio and for the next half an hour Maggie and Christine worked out their music schedule with the requests they had in from the previous day. Christine was an eager helper, pulling out all the CDs they needed and stacking them in order, which was just as well as Dougy had commandeered Maggie's lap.

He sat imperiously, his IV pole supporting his life-saving fluids close by, well used to adults indulging him. He leant his colouring book against the console and Maggie chatted to him, accepting the crayons he gave her and colouring where he pointed. Meanwhile she juggled Christine's questions and those of the volunteers as they wandered in and out on their way to the various wards in their bright Radio Giggle T-shirts.

Maggie knew the outside play area would be full of kids over the next couple of hours as those who could came down to see how a real radio show was run. They usually put callouts to their bed-bound friends and families and took part in the activities organised by the volunteers.

At four o'clock the programme got under way. Maggie and Dougy stayed in the studio and let Christine run the show. Dougy knew he had to be quiet and while he had his colouring book he was happy to sit without talking on Maggie's lap and draw. Radio Giggle never pretended to be a professional outfit, given that the shows were largely run by kids, but it never hurt to strive for excellence.

Maggie rubbed her face against his blond curls and inhaled the hospital-soap smell as she dropped a kiss against his scalp. Dougy had been born prem to a drug-addicted mother and had developed necrotising enterocolitis, necessitating the removal of a large portion of his non-viable bowel.

He'd been very ill for the first year of his life and had been transferred from NICU to PICU at three months of age for ongoing management. He now had short-gut syndrome, which meant he didn't have enough bowel length to absorb his food and had to be fed intravenously through a permanent line.

He'd been in hospital virtually all his life due to his condition and he made regular appearances in PICU with various infections which, due to his compromised immune system, usually knocked him for six. His last stay had been a few months ago during winter for bilateral pneumonia.

He looked like all kids with severe malabsorption disorders. Skinny arms and legs and a protruding stomach. While long-term parenteral nutrition was life-saving for Dougy it did have its side effects, and Maggie knew liver damage was a major contributing factor to Dougy's pot belly. She could feel its rounded contours through the thin cotton of his hospital-issue pyjama shirt and dropped another kiss on his head.

'So this is where the party's at.'

Maggie would have jumped a mile in the air had Dougy not been weighing her down as Nash

Reece's voice intruded into the studio bubble. What the…? Was the man stalking her?

'Dr Reece!'

Maggie blinked as Christine jumped up from the console, reefing her headphones off smiling crazily at him. She turned to see him standing in the doorway in dark chinos and another checked shirt. A young child sat on his hip, pulling at a lopsided bandage wrapped around its head. Nash looked natural, at ease with the child and her stomach did that strange flopping thing again.

Nash smiled at the teenager. 'Hello, Christine.' Then he turned to Maggie, looking smoking hot in her tight black denim Capri pants and her red Radio Giggle top fitting snugly across her breasts. 'Hello, Maggie from ICU.'

Maggie felt heat creep into her cheeks as his eyes roved all over her body.

'This little munchkin says his name is Brodie and he wants to say hello to everyone on ward three,' he announced to Christine, dragging his eyes off Maggie.

'Bring him over here.' Christine smiled, holding out her arms and waggling her fingers. 'I'll help him. Then we can do your interview.'

Maggie looked at him dumbly as Christine settled the little one on her lap. 'You're the interviewee?'

Nash chuckled. 'You think I'm going to tank?'

Maggie felt more fire in her cheeks. 'Of course not.' *It was hardly* Meet the Press. She'd just wished she'd known. She hadn't asked Christine about the interview because she'd assumed it was going to be one of the other inpatients as usual. 'How'd that come about?'

He shrugged. 'I've been dropping in from time to time and Christine asked if she could interview me.'

Nash had been dropping in to Radio Giggle? 'Oh,' she said.

'What about you? You help out here much?'

Maggie shrugged. 'From time to time.'

'Hey,' Christine said, butting in. 'That's not true. Don't listen to her, Dr Reece.' She pointed to a series of framed photos on the wall above the console, several of them starring Maggie. 'Ross says Maggie was the driving force behind Radio Giggle and that it wouldn't even exist without her.'

Nash cocked his head back and looked at the enlarged snaps. A younger-looking Maggie with headphones on, sporting a wedding band and grinning at the camera caught his eye. And another with Maggie helping a very official-looking gent in a suit cut a ribbon across the doorway behind him.

He whistled. Yesterday he'd seen her as the efficient PICU nurse and today he'd seen her in another light. While his libido saw her as a gorgeous, sexy woman, the evidence of his eyes told him Maggie was definitely more than a pretty face.

Dougy finally looked up from his picture. 'Dr Reece,' he called, and Maggie was spared from the frank curiosity in Nash's face.

'Hey, Dougy.' Nash crossed the small distance

and crouched beside Maggie. Doug had been his patient during his medical rotation. 'How you doin', mate?'

Dougy held up his colouring book. 'I'm colouring in a princess. Isn't she pretty?'

Nash nodded. 'As a picture.'

'She's not as pretty as Maggie, though.'

Nash, fully aware that his knee was almost brushing her thigh, glanced at her face and smiled as Maggie's cheeks bloomed with another flush of red.

Out of the mouths of babes.

'No,' he agreed, his gaze holding hers. 'No one's as pretty as Maggie.'

There was a strange couple of seconds when everyone else in the room ceased to exist. And it was in that moment that Maggie saw the difference in Nash. He wanted her, she could tell, but there was something more there. Respect maybe. Whatever it was it was infinitely more seductive than flirty Nash of yesterday.

'Okay,' Christine said, pulling the earphones

away again while simultaneously jiggling her new assistant on her lap. 'After this song you're up, Dr Reece. Are you ready?'

Nash reluctantly flicked his gaze from Maggie to Christine, giving the teenager his full attention. 'Ready when you are.'

Maggie watched Christine blush under Nash's gaze. It was apparent the girl had a massive crush on him, a fact of which he was obviously aware as he carefully navigated the interview. He was charming and gentlemanly to a fault, and everything a teenager hooked on Jane Austen could ever hope for, but Maggie could tell he was constantly aware of the boundary.

He spoke about growing up on a huge cattle property hundreds of kilometres west of Sydney in rural New South Wales and taking his school lessons via a radio through the School of the Air and mustering cattle in a helicopter.

'And why did you decide to become a doctor?' Christine asked.

Maggie, who'd been preoccupied with colouring a pink flower, looked up at the question. Christine had her back to Maggie but Nash was facing her. She noticed that at some stage Brodie had switched laps and was once again cuddled into Nash's side. She wouldn't have thought it possible but he looked more masculine, more appealing. Their gazes locked as he answered.

'My sister was sick a lot when we were kids and she had to go to Sydney frequently for treatment because there just weren't the services in the bush. I promised her then I'd become a doctor and change it.'

Maggie noticed the lightness to his voice and the smile he flashed Christine as he broke eye contact with her, but it was too late. For a brief moment she'd seen a vulnerability in his gaze as he'd spoken about his sister that called to her more than any amount of sexual attraction. And who could resist a fervent boyhood promise?

'You told me the other day that Radio Giggle was a life-saver. What did you mean by that?'

Maggie gaped at the very grown-up question.

Forget community radio, Christine was heading for a career with *60 Minutes*.

'The hospital in Sydney where Tammy… stayed had its own kids' radio station. My sisters and I used to ring up and put in requests for her. She listened every day, she said it helped her miss home a little less.'

Goose-bumps broke out on Maggie's arms at the streak of raw emotion in Nash's not-quite-steady voice. His family had obviously been close and the connection with his ill sister through a hospital radio station, no matter how far in the past, clearly still resonated with him.

She'd never thought of that aspect of Radio Giggle before, more concerned with its diversionary attributes. But as a way for inpatients to feel connected to home, it was extraordinarily touching and she was proud all over again to be part of such a great organisation.

'Do you have a special request for us today, Dr Reece?'

Brodie started to grizzle and Nash shifted him

to the other hip and jiggled him a little. 'I sure do. I'd like to hear "Puff the Magic Dragon." It was Tammy's favourite.'

Maggie was pleased for Dougy and her enforced activity as the mournful strains of 'Puff' filtered through the studio. She gripped the crayon hard, the goose-bumps multiplying.

'Thanks, Dr Reece,' Christine enthused, pulling her headphones off.

Nash smiled and stood. Brodie was becoming more fractious, rubbing his eyes. 'No probs.' He started to sway as Brodie's grizzling became louder. 'Better get this little one back to the ward.'

Christine nodded. 'See you later.'

He nodded to the teenager then looked down at Maggie, who was colouring in studiously. 'See you, Maggie.'

Maggie looked up, unprepared for the picture Nash made as he swayed with bandage-headed Brodie. He was lean and sexy and utterly endearing. Yesterday she had thought how totally out of his league she was but today, child on hip, amidst the background chaos of Radio Giggle, he looked totally down-to-earth. Easily within reach. Temptingly so.

'Bye,' she dismissed, returning her attention to Dougy almost immediately.

She gripped the crayon harder as his sexy chuckle lingered in the studio well after he'd gone.

If she was ever granted the use of a magic wand for even just a few seconds, Maggie would use it to completely annihilate night duty from existence.

She hated it. With a passion.

Her first night in particular. So, she wasn't in the best of moods the next night when she switched off her ignition and climbed out of the car beneath a star-studded sky. Ten hours stretched before her and she yawned. Not a good sign!

Oh, she knew once she actually walked through the doors and greeted her fellow sufferers she'd be fine—it was the thought that was the most depressing. And the older she got the harder they were to get over. Back in her student days she'd bounce straight back. Twenty years later it took her a good couple of days to get over a run of nights.

After communal handover in the tearoom Maggie was allocated bed three and took bedside handover from Ray, the nurse who'd been looking after Toby Ryan since his admission to the unit at lunchtime.

Toby was a three-year-old boy who'd been born with a rare hereditary haematological disease. He'd been in and out of hospital most of his brief life, undergoing a multitude of different therapies in a bid to cure him. When everything had failed a bone-marrow transplant had been his only option and he was now fifty days post-procedure.

But not out of the woods. Unfortunately nothing had gone smoothly for little Toby and his chest X-ray had deteriorated in the last few days and was looking very pneumonic. He'd been started on antibiotics and had had sputum collected for analysis, but it had become obvious that morning that he required closer monitoring and further respiratory support so he'd been shifted to PICU.

She watched her patient carefully, noting even in his sleep he was using the accessory muscles in his chest to help him breathe. The sound of high-flow oxygen whooshing through his face mask and filling the attached plastic reservoir bag was surprisingly loud in an already noisy environment.

He was as cute as a button with tight black curls crowning his head, clutching a raggedy-looking teddy bear that was missing an eye and half an ear. He was wearing only pyjama pants, leaving his upper half exposed. Maggie frowned. He was working really hard, which was concerning especially considering his state of slumber.

Maggie did her start-of-shift checks and nursing assessments. Linda, the nurse in charge of the shift and a close friend, was setting up bed four for a retrieval patient when Maggie asked her to check some drugs shortly after. Then

Toby's mother, Alice, returned and Maggie chatted with her for a while.

It was a good couple of hours before Maggie had the chance to sit down and read back over Toby's notes. The PICU had electronic charting, with each bedside having its own computer terminal. Maggie sat at hers and read back through her patient's history. She noted that Toby's cousin had died from the same condition only last year.

She looked up from the screen and took in Alice dozing by her son's bed, his hand in hers. Maggie couldn't even begin to imagine how scary it must be for her and the rest of Toby's family.

The night settled into a familiar rhythm. Toby slept and held his own. Around her the other patients were behaving themselves also. The everyday noises of the unit didn't register as Maggie went about her work. The low hum of machines, the beeping and trilling of monitors, the slurp of suckers and the variety of alarms attached to the technology-saturated environment formed a continuous background drone.

Collectively they were as familiar to Maggie as the sound of her own breath, the beat of her pulse. And subconsciously she registered what each of them were. She knew which ones to worry about and which ones to ignore. And even deeply involved in other tasks, she knew instantly when something sounded different.

Linda relieved Maggie for her first break. She returned half an hour later, coinciding with the arrival of the retrieval patient. Two paramedics pushed the gurney accompanied by a wardsmen and Gwen, the retrieval nurse.

But none of them held her interest or her gaze. Maggie could focus only on the other member of the party making their way towards her.

Nash Reece.

What the hell? What was Nash doing here? Wasn't it bad enough that visions of the man with a child on his hip had been in her head like a recurring nightmare since yesterday? His gaze locked with hers as the gurney rolled past and he winked at her.

'Hello, Maggie Green.'

Maggie stared at him, not even registering that he now knew her last name as her brain grappled with how exactly he came to be doing a PICU retrieval. Or at least it was trying to underneath the surge of one hundred per cent octane lust that had flooded her system and threatened to overload her circuits.

The man looked incredible. His hair was mussy in a too-sexy-to-be-true fashion, no doubt aided by the in-flight helmet. The navy-blue shirt of the retrieval uniform fitted snugly across his broad shoulders and chest, the pocket announcing his position as Doctor in vibrant red stitching. The cuffs were rolled back to reveal those strong forearms dusted with blond hairs.

Flaunting propriety, he wore a pair of faded jeans instead of the matching navy trousers. They clung in all the right places and Maggie found herself wondering what he'd look like in nothing but the jeans.

'I'll shut this across, Maggie, so we don't wake Toby,' Linda said.

Maggie nodded mutely and watched as the concertinaed divider between beds three and four shut out not only the spill of light but also Nash Reece and those damn distracting Levi's.

Trying to concentrate on her work now was utterly useless. The voices next door were muted but she seemed finely tuned in to every low rumble or murmur that was distinctly Nash. Luckily Toby continued to sleep and although his effort remained the same, he still appeared to be coping.

An hour later, as Maggie typed her username and password into the computer to sign for a drug, she felt Nash's presence behind her like the heat from a nuclear power plant.

'MMG,' he mused, reading over her shoulder. It had taken him a few days to get a handle on the electronic charting and there was probably a heap of features he'd yet to work out, but he did know that all the staff usernames consisted of their initials. 'What's your middle name, Maggie Green?'

Maggie ignored him, refusing to turn and acknowledge his query. It was none of his business.

Nash moved so he was standing in front of her, one tanned elbow and one lean hip propped against her mobile computer table. 'Is it May? Are you a "Maggie May"? Was your mother a Rod Stewart fan?'

Maggie thanked her lucky stars for the relative dimness of the room as he crooned the opening notes of the well-known song.

'Yes. I know what you meant,' she said cutting into his surprisingly good baritone not sure she could stand being serenaded with that particular song about an illicit love affair between a younger man and an older woman. 'I was named May after my grandmother,' she said frostily. 'I'm *older* than the Rod Stewart song.'

Nash chuckled. 'I've never met a woman so keen to talk up her age.'

Maggie shrugged with as much nonchalance as she could muster. She couldn't help it if the twenty-somethings he dated had issues with getting older.

'I guess I'd better get used to it seeing as how I'm working here for the next three months.'

Maggie took a moment to reel in the leap of her pulse. *Three months?* Maggie frowned as a sudden realisation hit her. 'You knew!' she accused. 'The other day…at lunch…yesterday… you knew you were coming here.'

Nash smiled. 'Guilty.'

Maggie looked into his utterly guiltless face. 'You might have told me.'

'And have you prepared?' Nash laughed. 'I like seeing you flustered, Maggie Green.' Nash suspected not much flustered her and the fact that he'd put her off balance three times now was the boost his ego needed in the face of her continued resistance.

Maggie took a breath, refusing to rise to his bait or let him see how the prospect of three months in his vicinity rattled her. 'So how'd you swing that? The current registrars are only halfway through their term.'

'A short-term position came up. Dr Perkins offered it to me.'

Maggie frowned. Dr Gemma Perkins, the PICU director, never offered reduced terms. *He must be bloody good.* 'Why only three months?'

'I've got a position at Great Ormond Street in January.'

Maggie blinked. *London?* It must be part of his great career plan. 'Good hospital,' she murmured. Still…*London?* She found it hard to believe how he'd survive in the environs of British medicine where suits and ties were mandatory. He'd changed from his retrieval top into a T-shirt, that combined with the faded fashion of his low-rider jeans, was the epitome of laid-back.

Did he even own a tie?

Nash grinned at her understatement. G.O.S.H. was a world leader. 'The best.'

She nodded. 'I worked there years ago.'

Nash couldn't resist. 'Back when you were my age?'

Maggie looked into his open flirty gaze,

humour skyrocketing his attraction tenfold. 'No. Back when I was first married. Twenty years ago. I do believe you must have been about ten at the time?'

'About that.'

Maggie shook her head at his unabashed reply. *He was never ten.*

'Well, I guess I'd better get my A into G,' Nash said, reluctant to leave. 'I'm sure Mac wants to be getting home.'

Tonight? He was working tonight? She gave an inward groan. She'd assumed he was just doing the retrieval and then leaving. *Great!* Now she had to add Nash Reece and his unsettling presence to her first-night blues.

Two hours later Maggie lay in the darkened break room on a mattress on the floor, cocooned in warm blankets from the blanket warmer, trying to sleep. But her thoughts kept turning to Nash Reece with his impossible blue eyes.

Damn it! She was supposed to be sleeping.

She had one precious hour to recharge her batteries and here she was staring at the ceiling with Nash's *I like seeing you flustered, Maggie Green* whispering its treachery into her subconscious.

After twenty minutes she admitted defeat, got up and headed for the tearoom, feeling tired and irritable. She was going to have to settle for bad late-night TV and a cup of tea instead. She was channel-surfing when Nash entered the room a little later.

'Couldn't sleep, Maggie?'

His voice purred around her and her irritation ballooned. It was all his fault she was going to feel like death warmed up in the morning.

'Are you watching that?' he asked, not waiting for her to answer.

Maggie passed him the remote control. There was nothing on. 'Not really.'

'Goodo.' He took the gadget and flicked it to a sport channel. 'Country versus city,' he said to her. 'I missed it this afternoon.'

'You can take the boy out of the country, hey?'

He grinned at her. 'Something like that.'

Maggie sipped her cup of tea for a few minutes while Nash watched the television. The silence between them was unsettling. Not that he looked unsettled but she sure as hell felt it. It was too… intimate.

'So where exactly is home?' she asked.

'Far western New South Wales. The family owns a couple of hundred thousand acres.'

'You're a long way from your roots. I thought country boys hated the city?'

Nash hooted. 'Are you kidding? I love the city. I may be a country boy at heart but I feel like a kid in a lolly shop here. Don't get me wrong, I love getting down and dirty and dusty…' Nash paused as he watched Maggie's knuckles grow white around her mug. He knew she wasn't as indifferent to him as she pretended. 'But I love the theatre and the shopping and the night life.'

Maggie swallowed a snort. She just bet he liked the night life. She just bet he fitted right in and the girls in the clubs drooled over his strange mix of metro-sexual hottie and country-boy charm.

He was going to adore London. London was certainly going to *adore* him. 'So you're converted?'

'It'll do for now.'

'Ah. Your great career plans? Your path? Tell me about it.' This was good, they were chatting. Like two normal, reasonable adults. No vibe, just polite small talk.

Nash shrugged. 'Become the best damn paediatrician in Australia and then take myself back home. The bush is notoriously underresourced and underfunded. I want to start up a flying paed service.'

Maggie shouldn't have been surprised by that, given the stuff he'd talked about yesterday during his interview. His childhood promise to his sister. But she was. She couldn't have been more surprised if he'd said he was going to drop out of medicine and become a drag queen.

When he'd talked about being married to his

career the other day and finding out about London
tonight she'd assumed it was for some hotshot,
high-profile calling. To discover he was staying
true to his boyhood promise was stunning.

Nash Reece, the charming flirt who'd made it
clear he wanted her, had been pretty irresistible.
Nash Reece, honourable doctor with a selfless
purpose born from his sister's illness, was completely irresistible. She'd caught a glimpse of
this man yesterday in the studio. And she was
looking at the rest of him now.

'Your sister must be very proud of you,' she
murmured.

Nash shrugged. 'I'm sure she would be if she
was alive.'

Maggie stilled as a sense of dread washed over
her. Nash's features had become shuttered. 'Oh,
Nash. I'm sorry.'

'It's fine,' he dismissed. 'She had leukaemia. I
was eight. She was ten. It was a long time ago.'

'I'm sorry, I just assumed yesterday…you
didn't say,' she ended lamely.

'I didn't think it was appropriate to broadcast my sister's death on a kids' radio show in a children's hospital.'

'No,' she murmured. 'I suppose not.'

He was silent for a moment as the overwhelming rawness of that time came back to him. He didn't often talk about Tammy. Maybe the interview yesterday had sparked the memories again but he found himself wanting to tell Maggie about it.

'She died in the city because there weren't the appropriate support services at home to help with palliative care. Having to make long trips into Sydney was a drain on our family life and my parents' finances. Being separated from Tammy a lot of the time was really, really hard on the rest of us. We missed her.'

Maggie nodded. 'I can imagine.'

He looked at her, compassion swirling in the fudge-brownie depths of her eyes. It was nice not to have to explain the true impact of that to someone. The PICU got its share of oncology patients and he knew Maggie would understand the true horrors of the illness.

'It took a long time for Mum and Dad to get over it. I mean, they tried hard…for the rest of us, but they were just…sad.'

'Of course they were,' she murmured. 'I'm sure you all were.'

Nash looked at her, seeing not only compassion but respect. Suddenly she didn't look at him like he was an annoying bug buzzing around. Or a child, to be tolerated or humoured. Suddenly she looked as if she was taking him seriously. Not dismissing him with a pat on the head. She was looking at him like he was a man.

Sort of like how he'd felt about her yesterday when he'd discovered her background with Radio Giggle. Instantly she'd become a three-dimensional entity and he'd had to face that there was more than a physical trigger to the tug he felt when they were together.

He didn't know whether to be pleased by this development or to get up and leave the room.

There was something in her gaze that saw deep inside him. Something he knew for sure would demand more from him than he was usually prepared to give.

The television erupted. The crowd cheered and the commentator's voice rose an octave or two as one of the country team made a mad dash for the goalpost. Nash was grateful for the diversion and he dragged his gaze from hers and feigned interest in the game.

Maggie was also pleased for the distraction. Things had suddenly gotten quite intense and it was the last thing she wanted. Writing Nash off as a frivolous jack-the-lad had made it easier to ignore the attraction between them. But his family tragedy and dedication to his career had added a whole further dimension. A fully fleshed-out Nash Reece was going to be much harder to ignore.

'Well, my time's up.' Maggie stood. Actually, she had another eight minutes but she really needed to get away.

Nash nodded, deliberately keeping his eyes trained on the television. Something had passed between them, making his interest in Maggie Green very unwise. He needed to give up on her pronto, because the Maggie who had just looked at him with compassion and respect in her eyes wouldn't be so easy to turn his back on come January.

And that he couldn't allow. There was London and then home. No woman had ever swayed him from his goal and he wasn't about to get tangled up with one who could.

So, there was chemistry. So, he wanted her. Maggie Green was off limits.

He'd better get used to it.

CHAPTER THREE

NASH SPENT THE next two weeks ignoring his attraction to Maggie. Something he never did. He'd learnt from his sister's passing that life was short and should be lived to its fullest. But during their talk the other night he'd realised Maggie was not the type of woman with whom he could indulge in a quick fling.

There was something about her that flashed a big red warning light at him. Maggie was a forever kind of woman. And he wasn't a forever kind of guy.

He had years left of his training to go, several in London and then back to the bush. Maybe one day, *maybe,* he'd find a nice country girl to settle down with, maybe have what his parents, his grandparents had, but he was certainly in no rush.

But then he made the fatal error of joining the staff for Friday night drinks and he knew he couldn't deny it any more. Two hours of watching her moist lips suck amber liquid out of long-necked bottles and he was wishing he was her beer. She was driving him to distraction. He had to have her—despite the warning light, despite knowing it was crazy.

He couldn't remember ever wanting a woman this badly.

Maggie lifted her gaze to his for a brief second before she hastily looked away and smiled at something Linda was saying. He knew she could feel the pounding of attraction growing out of control too. Louder than the noise of the juke box and the chatter all around them. It was as if the social situation, far removed from the hospital, had changed the boundaries between them.

She'd been slipping him furtive looks all evening when she'd thought he hadn't been watching and while it was dim inside her desire flared like a lighthouse beacon, beckoning him closer. Even though the rocks were treacherous and he risked being snagged, their attraction pulled at him like the undertow of a tsunami.

He needed another drink.

Maggie breathed a sigh of relief as Nash left the table. She'd felt the weight of his gaze all evening and it excited and terrified her in equal measure. She had an overwhelming feeling of inevitability and it sucked the breath out of her lungs.

He looked his usual laid-back sexy self tonight in faded jeans and a polo shirt the exact shade of his tropical-waters eyes. It touched all the right places on him and inside her. He looked good enough to sprinkle with sugar and eat with a spoon.

God, this was getting way out of hand. They'd spent a fortnight studiously avoiding each other. Oh sure, the zing between them was there but it was as if he'd decided to crank back the vibe. He didn't flirt. He was polite, friendly. And that suited her just fine.

In fact, she was very grateful for his detachment and returned it in the same spirit. But tonight it was if a channel of energy had opened up across the table between them, a portal visible only to them, and the bounds they'd subliminally put on their relationship had been sucked away.

Nash returned to the table with a glass of beer and looked directly at her, his gaze grazing her face before dropping to the V neckline of her T-shirt. He looked back up at her and Maggie could see the raw hunger in his eyes. She stood. She couldn't bear it any longer. If she didn't leave now she was going to drag him into the loo just to get it out of their system.

'I'm off,' she announced.

There was a chorus of protest but Maggie waved it all away.

'Me too.' Nash stood, leaving his untouched beer. 'Do you think you could give me a lift?' he asked, looking directly at her.

Maggie swallowed, hoping the heat between them wasn't as obvious to everyone else. 'I'm getting a taxi.'

'Good. We can share.'

Maggie saw the desire in his gaze light up his blue eyes with purpose and it scared her witless. But she nodded anyway.

There was a queue at the taxi rank and Maggie's heart belted along at triple time as they stood side by side, jostled by others in front and behind.

'What are we going to do about this, Maggie May?'

Maggie heard the murmur of his voice near her ear and knew they were standing at a crossroads. The wise thing to do would be to stick to her side of the path. But as she looked up into his face she knew she wanted him to kiss her more than she'd wanted anything in the last decade, and she knew she was powerless to resist.

Tonight, anyway.

They moved to the top of the queue and she

looked around at the people behind, relieved to see they were too engrossed in their own conversations to be paying any heed to theirs.

'One night,' she said, amazed at the steadiness of her voice as she took charge of her destiny to the pounding of her bongo-drum pulse. 'One night only.'

Nash's heart crashed to a brief standstill in his chest before galloping madly. He searched her gaze for a moment. He'd expected her to knock him back, to persist with her denial. But she was looking at him calmly. Intently. No doubts. No Maggie of old. Just double chocolate fudge brownie eyes sucking him in, tempting him further.

And one night was good. Enough to quench the attraction but not for it to be misconstrued as anything other than two adults having a good time. Perfect. 'Works for me.'

Maggie breathed again. 'How far away do you live?'

'Ten minutes.'

'I'm closer.'

A taxi pulled up. 'Get in,' he said, opening the door.

A trill of lust squirmed through her abdomen at what she'd just initiated, and her hands trembled a little before her legs kicked into action. She hesitated at the door for a moment then Nash smiled at her like he already knew all her secrets and wild horses wouldn't have kept her out of the cab.

She slid across the seat, giving the driver her address, aware of Nash like she'd never been aware of anyone before as he scooted across the seat. He moved in close, draping his arm along the back of the seat, crowding her, surrounding her.

He nuzzled her ear and her neck, and when his hand skimmed her thigh, slowly creeping up one denim-clad leg, Maggie almost whimpered out loud she was so turned on. She should have been mortified that they were necking like teenagers but she was so utterly caught up in his heat and his smell and the sexual squall lashing her insides and scrambling her thought processes, she couldn't have cared less.

She wanted to feel his lips on her so badly she turned her face towards him, her mouth seeking his as she clutched at his shirt, fisting it. 'Nash,' she whimpered as his lips brushed lightly against hers. Soft, teasing. She clutched his thigh, trying to anchor herself in the maelstrom.

Nash felt her desperate whimper right down to his toes and knew exactly how she felt. He wanted to tear her clothes off right here and now, push her back against the seat and have his way with her, audience or not.

And if he deepened the kiss that's exactly what would happen. 'Shh, Maggie,' he whispered, kissing her forehead, her eyes, her cheek. 'Nearly there.'

Maggie made a sound of protest deep in her throat. How could he be so controlled when she was practically blind with lust? His thigh felt thick and powerful beneath her hand and she massaged it convulsively, trying to claw back her breath, her sanity.

Nash clasped his hand over hers as it moved

higher. God, didn't she know he was holding on by a thread? He placed his forehead against her cheekbone, forcing himself to slow it down, to think practically for a moment while he still had the chance.

'Have you got condoms at your place?' He had two in his wallet but no way was that ever going to be enough. They were going to make love all night long. They might have to stop somewhere and get a supply.

Maggie only just heard the question over the thrumming of the pulse in her ears. She shut her eyes, desperately trying to gather her thoughts. *Protection, Maggie, protection— think!* It had been too many years since it had been an issue.

'Oh…er…yes.' Think. Think. She did have some somewhere. 'I have a…a box…' Where. *Where?* 'In… in my bedside drawer.'

Nash pressed a kiss to her temple and moved his hand further up her leg. 'I hope it's full.'

Maggie strained to think again. 'Well, it's been

a while since I've used any but I'm pretty sure they've barely been touched.'

Nash felt strangely satisfied by the admission. 'Good. We're going to need every one.' And he kissed her full on the mouth.

Maggie's head spun as she clung to his chest and opened her mouth to his deep, wet kiss, moaning low in her throat.

'Er…' the driver coughed. 'We're, uh, here.'

Nash pulled his mouth away, groped in his back pocket for his wallet, passed the driver twenty dollars and dragged Maggie out of the car. 'Keys.'

Maggie, too lust-drugged to co-ordinate herself, handed him her purse and clung to his hand as his long legs strode up the path. They reached the front door and she leaned her hip against it watching through a sexual haze as Nash sorted through her keys.

The subdued light from a sensor light spilled across his profile and down the tanned column of his neck as the keys jingled. She leaned forward, the flutter at the base of his neck too tempting to resist. She pressed her lips to it, his stubble grating against them. The smell of man enveloped her and she inhaled deeply, his aroma making her dizzy. She moved her lips higher to the ridge of his windpipe.

Nash, having trouble finding the right key, shut his eyes as her tongue caressed the path of his carotid pulse. He reached for her hip, the contours beneath moulded perfectly by the tightness of denim. 'Maggie,' he moaned.

Their lips sought and met and opened and he backed her against the door, his body covering hers wanting to feel every inch of her against him, the keys forgotten. Her mouth was warm and wet and inviting, and when she moaned and shoved her fingers into his hair he pushed his thigh between her legs and ground it against her.

Maggie gasped at the surge of pure desire that scorched her, and rubbed herself against the thick wedge of hard muscle sandwiched at her centre. She grabbed his shirt, faint from need. Her fingers brushed the contours of his chest and he felt warm and vibrant and very, very male.

'Inside,' she croaked as his lips left hers to nibble down her neck and his hand stroked a sinful tattoo on her hip.

Nash hauled himself away with difficulty, his breath harsh in the still night. 'Right,' he said handing her the keys. 'Open the bloody door.'

He stood aside for her and she took the heavy keyring from him, turning to insert the front door key into the lock. She pushed it in but then Nash's lips were at her neck and his heat was at her back and she shut her eyes as her head lolled to the side to give him better access.

'Damn it, Maggie,' he whispered against the arch of her neck, his lips caressing her heated skin, 'open the door.'

Maggie fumbled with the key as her flat-lined brain grappled with even the most basic task. Her fingers, heavy and useless, fumbled with the lock. But then the key turned and the door was opening to them, and then they were on the other side in the dark, fumbling for each other. She was turning and he was reaching and they fell into each other like lovers starved for an eternity of the other's touch.

She reefed his shirt out of his jeans as he toed off each of his shoes. He pulled at her shirt, lifted it over her head and flung it to the floor. She returned the favour, feeling his muscles shift beneath her fingers as she reached the good stuff.

She couldn't ever remember feeling this desperate, this crazed, this focused on getting a man naked. She must have with her ex, in the beginning before conception sex and fertility treatments had derailed their lives. Back when sex had been for fun instead of procreation. Like this.

Nash fumbled with the clasp on her purple lace half- cup bra. 'Off,' he growled. 'Take it off.'

Maggie felt her pelvic floor muscles seize at his rough demand. No. It had never been like this with Pete. Never.

The light from a streetlamp filtered in through a nearby open doorway and Nash's frustration was well rewarded as she unclasped the bra and her naked breasts fell free, bathed in milky light. They were rose-tipped and heavy, her skin lush and creamy.

'Oh, my,' he whispered, taking a moment to just look at her.

Maggie blushed at his reverent exclamation and part of her wanted to cover herself beneath his hungry gaze. But another part wanted to lean back against the doorframe and wantonly arch her back like an old-time film starlet. Blood roared in her ears as his eyes explored every inch of her.

'And those,' he said, his voice rough as he pointed at her jeans.

He watched as Maggie unzipped, peeled the denim down her legs and stepped out of their confines. A scrap of matching purple lace underwear hid the last piece of her from him and Nash reached out to her hip. 'You're even more beautiful than I imagined, Maggie May, and I've been imagining this…a lot.'

Maggie felt the heat in her cheeks intensify. Beneath his gaze she felt beautiful. She didn't feel ten years his senior. She didn't feel like a Mrs Robinson tutoring him in the art of a love. Or an infertile divorcee, somehow less of a woman. She felt his equal, his partner and *all woman.*

She closed the distance between them, her nipples tightening as they grazed against the light smattering of blond chest hairs. She rose on her tippy-toes, twined her fingers in his hair and pulled his head down so their lips met.

His mouth was hot against hers, sliding fire across her lips and into her mouth and beyond to her stomach, her breasts, her belly. Her soul. She opened for him, wanting more, welcoming the heat with more of her own. Fighting fire with fire.

His tongue tangoed with hers and she dug her nails into his shoulders, pushing closer, whimpering her need. His big hands smoothed over her back, drawing circles over her shoulder blades and ribcage, trailing fire there too as he anchored her to him. She could feel his arousal pressed into her stomach and she pushed against it, aching to touch it, for it to be inside her.

Her hand went to his belt and Nash groaned. 'Hold on,' he murmured, scooping her up, gathering her into his chest and looking for a place to get horizontal.

'End of the hallway,' Maggie murmured, her lips at his ear, her arms clinging to his neck.

Nash didn't need any more direction, striding down the passageway and pushing the door open with his knee. He crossed to the bed and lowered her until she was stretched out before him. He stood and looked. Just looked.

She was beautiful.

Maggie felt her cheeks grow hot as his gaze travelled over her with a thoroughness that left her breathless. 'Nash.' She squirmed.

His gaze trekked back to her face. She was flushed and had pulled her bottom lip between her teeth. 'God, Maggie, you're gorgeous.'

The awe in his voice was a huge turn-on and

she could feel her nipples hardening beneath his frank gaze. 'I think one of us has too many clothes on,' she murmured.

'You're right.' He reached down, ran his finger under the edge of her lace knickers and tugged.

'Not quite what I had in mind.' Maggie rolled her eyes but lifted her hips.

Nash grinned as he tossed the article on the floor behind him. 'Perfect,' he whispered.

Maggie was on fire. His eyes roamed over her nakedness like it was his own private playground and again she was struck by the urge to arch her back. Her blood thickened, simmered, boiled. 'Your turn.'

Nash took another moment to commit her curves to memory before reaching for his jeans, unzipping and stepping out of them.

Maggie was speechless. He stood before her clad only in his underwear with all the perfection of a marble statue overlayed with the flesh and blood of a warm, vital man. He was amazing, his washboard abs well defined and gloriously bronzed. His broad shoulders and chest even more impressive from her reclining position.

'God, you have a magnificent chest.'

He chuckled. 'You've got a pretty nice one too.'

A trail of blond hair bisected his abdominal musculature, wisping down behind the band of his underwear, and her fingers itched to follow it.

Maggie vaulted upright, their gazes locked. She raised a hand and placed it flat against his stomach, feeling his muscles there react. She let it slide down slowly until it was resting on his waistband. 'These now,' she requested huskily.

Her gaze zeroed in on the erection his underpants were barely restraining, and he felt a punch to his gut as she moistened her lips. He watched as if in slow motion as she lifted a tentative finger and traced the thick ridge.

'Maggie.' His warning was half whisper, half groan.

She looked up into his face, dragging her gaze from the bulge in his pants, dropping her hand from the tantalising contours. 'You're magnificent everywhere.'

Nash was mesmerised by the desire in her eyes, by the way she looked at him like he was the only man on earth. He lifted his hand to her cheek and stroked it, his fingers pushing into her hair, brushing at her fringe, cupping the back of her head. Her lips shone in the semi-dark and he wanted some of them.

'Lie back, Maggie,' he whispered.

Maggie fell back as he asked and she watched as he stepped out of his underwear and she was finally able to see him in all his glory. She exhaled a ragged breath at his proud length, ready, eager before him. He put a knee on the bed beside hers and she held her arms out to him, exulting in the knowledge that all that hardness would soon be inside her.

Nash lay on his side, propped on his elbow, looking down at her. Their gazes locked and he traced the planes of her face with his index finger. Over her eyelids, across her cheekbones and the moist seam of her lips. He continued lower, holding her gaze as his finger traced down her throat, dipping into the hollow, down her chest, over her stomach to her belly button. Then he reversed the process.

'Nash,' she whimpered against his finger as it trailed across her mouth.

He pushed his finger gently against her mouth to still her protest, pausing to study her lips. He rubbed his thumb over the bottom one and then the top, smearing the moisture all over.

'Nash.' Maggie was trembling with want, his intense gaze zeroed on her mouth incredibly erotic.

'Shh,' he whispered, mesmerised by their movement, by how they looked all swollen and moist from his ministrations. He just had to taste them.

When Nash finally lowered his head it was for an agonisingly slow exploration of her mouth. Maggie tried to deepen it, to open beneath him and draw his tongue inside her mouth but he pulled back and smiled at her. 'Patience, Maggie. We've got all night.'

She shivered at the promise in his voice, in his eyes, accepting the teasing stroke of his lips against her again with an eagerness that bordered on shameless. The kiss slowly deepened and Maggie moaned as his tongue finally touched hers.

His hand spread its own joy, lightly stroking down her neck and her chest to her breasts. Her nipples beaded at the light play of his palms over them and she arched her back and moaned into his mouth as he rubbed them into unbearably tight pebbles.

Nash dragged his mouth from the drugging kisses of hers, eager to taste the engorged tips. He'd dreamt about it but already knew it was going to far exceed his expectations. He kissed down her throat, feeling the whimpering noises coming from her as they vibrated against his lips.

When his tongue flicked out to touch one turgid peak he felt her whole body tremble and when he sucked it fully into the hot cavern of his mouth she dug her nails into his back so hard he knew there'd be blood.

'Nash!' Maggie almost lifted off the bed as her stomach clenched in ecstasy.

Nash smiled against her skin and paid the other breast equal homage, eliciting another fevered response. Her reaction stoked the fire in his loins ever higher and he felt a surge of animal power that he could turn her mindless with passion.

She was so reactive. Her skin goose-bumped wherever his breath meandered, tiny mewing noises slipped from her lips and she trembled beneath his touch. He'd never had such a responsive lover and it was incredibly arousing. It urged him to go further, push her higher, give her more, and he moved his hand lower to stroke down her belly as his mouth continued to feast on her breasts.

Maggie shook her head from side to side in utter mindless ecstasy. He had to stop. She couldn't take it any more. She was going to die from pleasure. He'd no sooner finish ravaging one turgid peak than he'd turn his attention to the other and her pelvic floor muscles would contract again.

'Stop,' she moaned as Nash switched sides again. 'They can't take any more.' She was close to delirious with lust. Mindless with passion. Treading that fine line between pleasure and pain.

Nash looked up from his feast. 'No.' His hand slipped lower, stroking her inner thigh.

'Nash,' she begged.

He smiled. 'Uh-uh. These…' he paused and looked down at her large breasts with their proudly erect nipples. 'Have been taunting me all night under that damn T-shirt—it's payback.' He dropped a quick, hard kiss on her mouth as his fingers stroked her slick entrance. 'Just lie back and enjoy.'

Maggie's eyes rolled back in her head as he found his target, pushing inside her at the same time his mouth reclaimed a nipple. Just when she'd thought more pleasure wasn't possible he proved her wrong and she arched off the bed as he inserted another finger and probed deep inside.

Through the haze of sensations she could feel his erection thick against her thigh and she reached for him, desperate to touch him as he was her. To feel the hot length of him. To hear him moan in mindless abandon and know that she was responsible. He batted her hand away and she growled her frustration. 'Nash—'

He cut off her protest with another hard kiss. 'Not yet,' he whispered against her lips, raising his head briefly before plundering her mouth and her body into submission.

If she touched him, he wasn't sure how long he'd last. He'd been fantasising about her, about this, for two weeks, and with the wild blend of her perfume and the sweet smell of her readiness intoxicating him, his control was tenuous at best.

His hand returned to the slick heat at her centre and her hips bucked convulsively. Her shudder as he stroked the tight nub there told him she was close and after numerous fantasies of her coming apart beneath him, he was hungry for the reality.

Nash broke away from her mouth. 'Condoms,' he whispered raggedly against her neck.

Maggie's blood felt like treacle, her brain waves practically at a standstill as she dragged herself back from the fireworks display that was going on in her head. 'Drawer closest to you,' she panted.

Nash reached across her, yanked the drawer open and blindly felt for the box. He located it, pulled out a foil packet and quickly tore it open with unsteady fingers as Maggie teased his throat with wet kisses.

'Now,' he said, covering her body with his. He paused for a second, looking down into her face, her fudge-brownie eyes glazed with passion, her mouth moist and slightly parted, their hips aligned, their hearts pounding together.

'Now,' Maggie whispered, her pelvis rising to meet his as he slid into her, stretching her, filling her, completing her. 'Yes,' she sighed, her hands gripping his shoulders as he rocked her into the bed.

'Yes,' he groaned as her heat enveloped him, seduced him, possessed him. He stilled, dropping his mouth to hers, kissing her deep and hard. He pulled away, resting his forehead against hers, breathing hard. 'I knew it was going to be like this.'

Maggie dragged in a ragged breath, aware only of his girth nestled against all the right places inside her. 'Like what?'

'Perfect.'

And he pulled out and pushed in, and pulled out and pushed in and the heat built everywhere as his biceps slicked with sweat and her brain went to mush and her lungs turned to liquid as her body was consumed by the heat. The heat of him. Of them.

The pressure built with each deep, measured thrust from his hips and it was like an itch, a bubble beneath her skin, building and spreading outwards, like a ripple in a pond growing larger.

Nash could feel her trembling and he gathered her close and whispered, 'Yes, Maggie, yes,' in her ear. Her first cry pierced him to the core and she tightened around him like a vice, her hips bucking, her chest arching.

'Nash!' Maggie was slammed from all directions by the powerful sensations of her orgasm and all she could do was hold on tight and ride the fallout.

Nash kept up the rhythm for as long as he could, staving off his own build-up as she broke around him. But her rhythmic contractions pulled at his resistance, sucked at his willpower, and he followed her over the edge, holding her close as they free fell through a quagmire of sensations that sucked and pulled and spun them around until they lay shattered and weary at the bottom.

CHAPTER FOUR

NEITHER OF THEM moved for several minutes as they waited for earth to right itself and their breathing to return to normal. Maggie shifted underneath him and Nash moved off her, rolling onto his back still dazed by a sexual energy with a kick more powerful than dynamite.

'Wow.'

Maggie laughed. 'Yes. Wow.'

They lay still, looking at the ceiling for a few more minutes, not touching, just breathing, languishing in a post-coital drowse, savouring the last vestiges of sensation lingering in their tissues.

Nash roused himself to go to the bathroom, a smile curving his mouth. It didn't last long. To his horror he discovered something that banished the smile and the lassitude in his bones in an instant. The condom had ruptured.

A fist slammed into his gut.

No. No. No.

His mind raced with a thousand dire scenarios. He looked at himself in the mirror. He should be looking sated, relaxed, instead of tense and frowning, and the urge to throw something at it almost overpowered him. He didn't want this night, what had just happened, diminished by contraception failure.

Or for it to be over before it had even really begun. Nothing like the spectre of pregnancy to kill a mood.

Damn it all to hell!

He stood in the doorway and watched her for a moment. She'd moved, pulled the covers down and got in the bed proper, the sheet pulled up to her hips. Her head was turned away from him and his gaze greedily devoured the contours of her breasts, the line of her neck and the way her stomach sloped down to her pelvis. He felt himself twitch and again felt annoyed that the night had come to a premature end.

Maggie stirred and turned her head. How long had she drifted off for? She focused in the dim light and spotted Nash standing in her en suite doorway, gloriously naked. Memories of that nakedness all over hers returned and she smiled at him. 'You're a long way away.'

Nash smiled back despite the situation. 'Easily fixed.'

She watched as he sauntered towards her, eyes glued to the easy movement of his tall, broad frame. Her gaze dropped lower as he neared and she could see he obviously had the stamina of a younger man.

He stopped by the side of the bed and looked down at her like he'd done earlier. But he seemed hesitant, tense. Maggie felt a trickle of dread brush her nape. Now his curiosity had been satisfied, was he having second thoughts? Was he trying to find the words to say he had to go?

She looked him straight in the eye. 'Regrets?'

'Oh, God, no, Maggie.' He sat on the bed and reached for her, pressing a kiss to her palm.

She withdrew it, a cold hand slowly wrapping her heart in icy fingers. 'Sounds like there's a but coming.'

Nash sighed. 'I'm sorry. *The condom broke.*'

Maggie blinked. And then blinked again as a wave of relief swamped her. The condom broke. That was all. He hadn't looked at her with their passion all burnt off and wondered what the hell he'd done. The condom broke.

She almost vaulted up and danced across the bed but one look at his shattered face told her he might not share her jubilation. Putting herself in his shoes she guessed that as a single footloose-and-fancy-free thirty-year-old man, it was probably the worst possible outcome from a night like this. But as an infertile forty-year-old woman, it didn't even rate on her list-of-things-to-worry-about.

Nash took her continuing silence as a bad sign. *Damn it! How quickly something good could turn so bad.*

'If you like, we can go and find a late-night chemist. I think there's one near the hospital. It's really best if you take emergency contraception as soon as possible after the incident.'

Maggie laughed. She couldn't help herself. Even when he looked at her like she'd grown a second head, she laughed.

Nash shut his eyes. Oh, God, she was hysterical. What a disaster. 'I'm so sorry,' he murmured.

She sobered at his look of utter misery. 'Hey.' She sat up, tucking her knees under her chin, hugging them close. They were very near now and she could see the concern marring the clarity of his blue eyes. 'It's okay.'

Nash looked at Maggie looking very calm and began to hope. 'You're on the Pill?'

She shook her head and watched the glimmer of optimism fade in his eyes. 'Come here,' she whispered.

Nash obliged, moving so he was sitting behind her, his legs spread, his back against the headboard, her body pulled into the shelter of his, her bottom snug against his crotch.

'We really should be thinking about going,' he said as she leaned back against him, shifting her head to a position of comfort under his chin and squirming her bottom against him. Her smell invaded his senses as he draped an arm across the front of her, pulling her closer. Her nipples beaded against his arm. The slope of her shoulder was close and he only had to drop his head to press a kiss there.

Maggie lightly stroked her fingers up and down the bulk of his biceps, thrilling in the way it twitched beneath her touch. 'Have you got any diseases I should know about, Nash?'

Nash arm's tightened at her bald question. He forced himself to relax, rubbing his face against her hair. It was a fair enough question. Condoms weren't just about pregnancy. 'Nope. I never have unprotected sex. Never. Ever. I give blood every three months so I know I'm clean.'

Maggie smiled, pleased at his vehement

response. Nash had started to trail his fingers up and down her shoulder, the movement dragging his arm across her, and she could feel her nipples growing harder beneath the erotic rub of his biceps. She shut her eyes, savouring the sensation.

'And you?'

Maggie's eyes fluttered open. 'Well, it's been a long time for me so I'm pretty certain there nothing to worry about.'

Nash kissed her head as things in his loins started to heat up. 'How long is long?'

Maggie almost didn't answer. Concentrating was difficult with his erection growing steadily against the small of her back, and she didn't think a virile young man would possibly understand her abstinence. 'About three years.'

He opened his eyes, his fingers stilling. Maggie had gone without sex for *three* years? He recommenced the stroking. 'Hell, Maggie, no wonder the condom broke. It's probably past its expiry date.'

Maggie laughed, relieved by his deliberate humour. But she wasn't fooled by it. Underneath his light words she could detect his horror at her non-existent sex life. Just one of the many differences between the two of them.

'You don't sound too upset by this,' Nash murmured after her laughter subsided. 'Aren't you worried about getting pregnant? Or is this a safe time in your cycle?'

Even as he said it he wished he could take it back. He was sounding like an ignorant teenager. There was never a safe time. God, he was a doctor, he'd spent six years at uni learning that!

Maggie shut her eyes, savouring the closeness of him, his warmth as she reached for the shield she hadn't needed in a long time. 'I'm infertile.'

Nash's hand stilled again. It had sounded casual but he could feel her tensing against him, her slouch less pronounced. 'Oh?'

'Two years of trying with my husband. Six years of IVF. Multiple attempts. Pregnancies none. Divorce one.'

He could hear the nonchalance she was forcing into her voice and was ashamed at the flood of relief sweeping through him. He didn't need to be a psychologist to know that Maggie had suffered. After a few moments he kissed her head and went back to trailing his fingers along her skin.

'That must have been hard,' he said carefully. He didn't want to betray his happiness in the face of Maggie's misfortune.

Maggie shut her eyes. It had been the most gut-wrenching decade of her life. No wonder she and Peter had crashed and burned. Years of her being a hormonal wreck, in debt to their eyeballs and having robotic sex devoid of any expression of love had led to an inevitable conclusion.

'Yes.' Made worse by Peter marrying again within the year and having three children in quick succession.

'Did they identify the problem?'

Maggie shook her head. 'No. Idiopathic infertility. After hundreds of tests and tens of thousands of dollars no one could tell me why.'

Sitting this close, knowing her like he now did, Nash could sense her deep, deep regret. He'd seen her with the kids at work. She would have been a good mother. 'I'm sorry.'

She turned her head and looked up at him, raising her palm to cup his face. 'It was a long time ago.' Hadn't he said that to her about his sister's death? She dropped her hand but continued to look at him. 'I take it from the overwhelming relief in your eyes that babies aren't on your agenda just yet?'

Nash shot her a sheepish grin. He felt like he'd dodged a bullet. 'Babies aren't on my agenda full stop.'

'Really?'

He nodded. 'Really.'

'Oh.' Maggie looked away.

He looked down at the top of her head. 'Is that so hard to believe?'

Maggie shrugged. 'You're training to be a paediatrician. I guess I assumed you liked them.'

'It's because of my profession I choose not to be a father. And my sister's death. I see the bad stuff that can happen to kids every day. I've witnessed it personally. Parents can do everything right and then, whammy! Out of the blue some horrible cancer or awful disease comes at you. I've seen how it tears families apart. How it tore at my own family for years. I lived through the death of my ten-year-old sister and I won't willingly set myself up for that kind of potential ever again.'

Maggie nodded. Obviously Nash's scars ran deep. Not that she could blame him. How often had she comforted herself with the fact that she would never know the agony of some of the mothers she'd been involved with over the years? Being infertile had been a cruel blow but Nash had a point. At least she would never know the even crueller blow of losing a child.

'Yes, losing a child must be deeply devastating.'

Nash rubbed his cheek against her hair. 'And I guess I have some old-fashioned beliefs. I don't think people should have children outside committed relationships. And I don't plan on committing to anything other than my career for many years to come.'

Maggie heard the grim certainty in his voice. It was easy to mistake Nash as a laid-back country boy but he was as driven and career focused as the most dedicated city doctor.

She shifted against him and wriggled a bit to get comfortable. 'It's good that you know what you want.'

Nash felt his erection swell back to life and chuckled. 'Well, I know what I want right now.' He dropped the arm draped around her shoulders and cupped her breasts in his palms.

Maggie sucked in a breath as a lust-tipped arrow shot straight to her core. 'I think it's the same as me,' she said, arching her back as he grazed his thumbs across appreciative nipples.

'Lucky for us I have two condoms in my wallet. Two new ones.'

Maggie looked up at him. 'I thought we just established there's no need.'

Nash dropped his head and kissed the tip of her nose as he kept up the massage of her breasts. The thought of being inside her with no barrier between them was tempting as hell. 'Old habits die hard.' He kissed her nose again. 'Just because you couldn't fall with your ex doesn't mean you won't with me.'

Maggie smiled at his youthful cockiness. 'You think your swimmers can manage what medical science couldn't?'

He grinned back at her. 'I don't want to risk it.'

Maggie sobered. Wow. He really, really, really didn't want kids. But then his right hand wandered from her breast, down her stomach and totally distracted her. She bit her lip and arched her back again. 'Are two going to be enough?'

Nash chuckled, his erection straining as he gazed down at her, her nipples taut, her stomach quivering beneath his touch. 'I'll get creative,' he murmured.

And he was. Very, very creative. All night long.

Two weeks later both Nash and Maggie found themselves on a run of nights together, the first time their shifts had coincided since their one-off night of passion. Maggie expected things to be awkward. At least a little. But he smiled at her in all his jeans-clad glory, a secretive I've-seen-you-naked-but-it's-okay smile when their gazes first met and she knew it was going to be all right.

Okay, yes, she'd spent two weeks reliving that night and all its wonder over and over in her head. She dreamt about it. About him. About his hands and what he'd done with them. His mouth and where he'd put it. And the pleasure he'd rained down on her in a frenzy of desire.

But they'd made a deal. One night only. And she had no intention of welshing on it. Even if sleeping in her bed with his smell embedded in her sheets and his touch, his taste embedded in her memories, was driving her crazy. What she had was a prime case of lust and she was fairly certain she wouldn't die from denial.

And the night didn't allow any time for either of them to psychoanalyse their night of hot sweaty sex. They hit the ground running and didn't stop. Maggie was in charge of the shift and a retrieval arrived as soon as handover finished. Billy Sugdeon, a five-year-old immersion, pulled from a back-yard fishpond with a ten-minute downtime.

The little boy was barely visible beneath the metallic space blanket as the paramedics pushed the gurney into one of the side rooms. Maggie and Gwen, Billy's assigned nurse, worked with Nash to get the blond-haired, blue-eyed darling unhooked from all the transport monitors, one ear on the handover. They transferred him to the bed and began hooking him up to their monitors.

'Are the parents here?' Maggie asked as the retrieval crew prepared to depart.

'Mum is. She's waiting in the parents' lounge. We told her you'd need an hour or so to get the little tyke settled but you'd go and get her when you were done.'

'Thanks.' Maggie nodded as she adjusted the ventilator settings.

Nash inspected the intra-osseous needle site. It had had been screwed into the patient's tibia when no other venous access could be found. The boy was pale and cold despite the space blanket, his heart rate a little too slow for his liking.

'Let's warm him up and get some lines in,' he said, flicking on the overhead warmer switch. 'We'll take him to CT after that.'

'You want some sedation running?' Maggie asked as Gwen went to get some blankets from the warmer.

'No. We'll let the retrieval stuff wear off and see what he does.'

Maggie and Nash worked together like they'd been doing it for years. Like they were professional colleagues only and their night of rapture had never happened. She assisted with several intravenous line placements, an endotracheal tube change and a chest X-ray.

Billy's limbs started to twitch as soon as the X-ray plate was removed from behind him.

'Midazalom,' Nash ordered.

Maggie administered the preprepared solution into Billy's central line and watched as the seizure stopped. It wasn't an unexpected development. Maggie knew that any injury to the brain, be it traumatic or hypoxic, usually resulted in some sort of seizure activity. She just hoped it was as the result of initial brain swelling and not a sign of more permanent damage.

'I'll write him up for a loading dose of phenytoin,' Nash said, accessing the computerised medication chart at the bedside console and ordering the anti-convulsant therapy.

Maggie checked the drug with Gwen. 'Why don't we get Mum in now? It'll give her some time before the CT scan.'

Nash nodded. 'I'll get her.'

Maggie watched surreptitiously a few minutes later as Nash approached the bedside with Billy's mother. He was talking in a low voice, his voice soothing to the obviously emotional woman. Her eyes were red-rimmed and her hands were visibly shaking.

As she got closer and saw her son looking small and helpless amidst all the medical equipment she pressed her hand to her mouth and fresh tears welled in her eyes. Maggie could see her hesitate, falter and then crumple.

'Whoa, there,' Nash said as the sobbing woman collapsed against him. He put his arm around her shoulders, holding her upright. 'Chair, Maggie.'

Maggie, well used to the emotional shock parents felt on seeing their children in a critical care environment, was two steps ahead of him and had the mobile stool behind the mother in an instant, allowing Nash to lower her gently. He knelt beside Billy's mother and shot a grateful smile at Maggie. 'Thanks,' he murmured.

Maggie nodded admiring his way with the overwrought woman reminding herself of their one-night-only deal. 'No problems.'

Gwen and Nash accompanied their patient to CT twenty minutes later and Maggie watched them go with a heavy heart. She shook her head and wondered how many blond-haired, blue-eyed immersions she'd looked after. She'd lost count over the years.

She looked through the glass window separating the two side rooms at the red-headed burns boy next door. Why were they always red-headed? She wondered if anyone had done a study on hair colour and its correlation to specific types of accidents?

She laughed out loud, the sound echoing in the empty room strewn with discarded packaging, used linen and multiple bits of medical plastic that had wound up on the floor. It seemed like such a trivial thought but anything that kept her mind off the horrifying prospect that Billy might be severely brain damaged was more than welcome. He and his mother had managed to touch her heart.

Maggie couldn't believe three hours had gone by. When she looked at the clock she was amazed to find it nudging midnight. She managed a quick breather to catch up with the other patients— there were two of concern.

Toby, who had been extubated yesterday after a few weeks of ventilation, appeared to be struggling again. And Ruby Wallace, a nine-year-old with a closed head injury thirty-six hours post-MVA, had a grumbling temp.

Thankfully Linda and another experienced nurse were helping to run the shift tonight and had been keeping an eye on these patients as well as the rest of the unit while managing all the breaks.

Billy returned from CT half an hour later. He'd warmed up, his heart rate had improved and he was reasonably stable. The CT showed global swelling but no specific areas of concern. Hopefully he was going to be one of the lucky ones.

No sooner had they got Billy settled back in when Linda entered the side room. 'Nash, Ray needs you. Toby's just not coping.'

Linda stayed to help Gwen get Billy sorted and Maggie went with Nash. The situation at bed three didn't look good at all and one look at Toby had Maggie pulling the resus trolley closer.

Toby, who usually beamed at anyone who came close to the bed, even with an endotracheal tube sticking out his nose, was looking exhausted, using all his accessory muscles in his chest again to help him breathe. He certainly had no energy left to smile. His oxygen sats were eighty-five on a hundred per cent rebreather mask and his arterial blood gas was abysmal.

'Shall we trial him on mask c-pap?' Maggie queried.

Nash nodded. 'I think so.' He popped his stethoscope in his ears and listened, not liking the decreased air sounds over his right chest. 'Let's get an X-ray too.'

Toby's father, Brett, was staying overnight and seemed very relieved when Nash explained to him that Toby would need to go back on non-invasive ventilation. Maggie could tell that watching his son struggle to breathe was increasingly distressing for the father too.

Toby wasn't having any of it, though, fighting the claustrophobic confines of the mask. The harder he fought, the more he taxed his respiratory system. He was also in a lather of sweat, which made maintaining a good seal on the mask very difficult.

The X-ray showed a marked deterioration from the morning's picture but no pnemothorax, as Nash had suspected. It took several doses of sedation to finally settle the boy with another blood gas finally showing an improvement in his gaseous exchange.

With the imminent crisis averted at bed three Maggie was able to grab her first cup of coffee. Considering it was almost three a.m. she was hanging for one. She made one for Nash too and brought it out to the central nurses' station, plonking it down beside him where he sat at the doctor's computer, making an electronic entry into Toby's chart.

Nash looked up. He hadn't had a chance tonight to think about their tryst but the smoulder in her fudge-brownie gaze put him straight back in her bed. 'Thanks,' he murmured.

Maggie's breath stuttered to a halt at the heat in his loaded gaze. Watching him in action tonight should have helped to put him firmly in the colleague category, but his calm capability, his decisive authority, his dedication to his job made him even more desirable.

She nodded and turned away. The night had been crazy and there was much to catch up on. She didn't have time to moon over his blond good looks. She sat at the computer console furthest away from him, planning to review all the patients' charts. She'd just clicked on the first one when Linda called her over to bed eight, where she was doing a meal relief.

'I don't like the look of her, Maggie.'

One look at Ruby Wallace and Maggie could understand Linda's concern. She was tachycardic, hypotensive and febrile. The little girl had been in a high-speed car accident two days ago. She'd been restrained but her head had still smashed sideways into the window, resulting in a large subdural haemorrhage. She'd had emergency neurosurgery to evacuate the blood but was still in a coma requiring ventilatory support.

'She's been grumbling along most of the day with this fever but just in the last twenty minutes she's spiked her temp and her heart rate. Her oxygen requirement has increased. Her lactate on her blood gas is rising and her blood pressure's bottoming out. I think she may be septic.'

Maggie nodded. 'Nash?' she called as she grabbed the resus trolley again.

Nash wasn't sure if it was because he was so attuned to her or whether it was the note of concern in Maggie's voice but he stood immediately, joining her and Linda at bed eight. He listened to their concerns, more than a little alarmed at the deterioration in Ruby's condition and the rising lactate.

'Yes. I think she may be septic too. Let's get some blood cultures and give her a ten per kilo bolus of colloid for her blood pressure to start with.'

Maggie accessed the arterial line for the blood while Linda hooked up the extra fluid.

'Her abdo's quite distended,' Nash mused, palpating the tense dome. They'd been treating Ruby for an illeus since admission due to her lack of bowel sounds and bruising from the seat belt. Abdominal ultrasounds had shown no acute trauma but they'd kept her nil by mouth while her gut recovered from the impact.

'Yes,' Linda agreed, 'I reckon it's blown up just in the last hour.'

Maggie added the blood to the culture bottles, a heavy foreboding settling in her bones. She reached up to the monitor to adjust the alarm settings as Ruby's heart rate climbed to one hundred and eighty. The little girl started to gag and cough and then vomited. Bilious liquid spilled from her mouth and nose, streaming down her face and over the sheets.

Maggie quickly whipped out the yankeur sucker and turning Ruby's head to the side to try to prevent aspiration, she suctioned the girl's airway while Linda aspirated the nasogastric tube. Alarms trilled all around them as Ruby's heart rate again breached the set limits.

'I'll call the surgical reg for a consult,' Nash said, walking briskly to the nearest phone.

Maggie wiped Ruby's face with a towel and used a couple more to sop up the excess stomach contents around her. Dr Hannah Oakland arrived fifteen minutes later as the second ten per kilo bolus was almost finished. Nash could see it was having no impact on the flagging blood pressure. 'Let's start some inotropes,' he ordered.

Maggie and Kylie, Ruby's nurse who had returned from her tea break, drew up some dopamine while Hannah and Nash consulted.

'You want an ultrasound?' Nash asked her

Hannah shook her head. 'I think we need to go in and have a look. I'll organise it. Where are her parents?'

'Mother's asleep in the parents' lounge,' Kylie volunteered.

Maggie, Nash, Linda and Kylie worked to sta-bilise Ruby for Theatre while Hannah talked to her tearful mother and gained consent for ex-ploratory abdominal surgery. Maggie averted her eyes as Ruby's mother stroked her daughter's hair, tears trekking down her face.

'It's okay, Rube,' she whispered, 'you're going to be okay.'

Even after fifteen years Maggie found it impossible not to become involved and she hoped desperately that Ruby's mother was right and her gut feeling was wrong.

The sky was lightening when they finally wheeled Ruby into the operating theatre at the end of the corridor. Maggie and Linda, who hadn't had a break yet, left Kylie to clean up the bed area confident that Ruby wouldn't be back until the end of their shift, maybe even after that.

Nash joined them in the tearoom and they all sat round staring into their coffees still a little dazed by rapid-fire events of the night. Sure, these nights happened every now and then but they were both physically and emotionally draining.

Linda drained her mug and stood. 'I'll go check on Kylie,' she said.

'You haven't finished your break yet,' Maggie protested.

Linda shrugged. 'I'm too wired to sit still.'

Maggie nodded. That happened sometimes. Adrenaline was vital to cope with the emergencies they'd had to face tonight but it did have its jittery side effects.

Linda departed and Nash was grateful to be left alone with Maggie. 'Are you okay?' he asked. She looked weary. Good, but tired around the eyes and tense around the shoulders.

'Sure,' she answered automatically, staring into the milky depths of her coffee. 'What about you?' she asked, remembering that Nash's sister had been about Ruby's age when she'd died.

'I'm okay.' He nodded. 'It's been a hell of a night.'

Maggie nodded, swirling the muddy liquid in the mug. That it had.

'I thought we'd pulled our last all-nighter,' he murmured.

Maggie flicked her gaze up from the drink. A small smile lifted the corners of his beautiful mouth and he looked sexy and inviting and she wanted to crawl onto his lap and snuggle her head into his neck.

She smiled back at him, her heart light for the first time this shift. She opened her mouth for a sexy rejoinder but a rattling up the corridor and the trilling of an alarm had her frowning instead. 'That can't be Ruby already?' She looked at her watch. 'It hasn't even been half an hour.'

But it was. Which could only mean two things. The problem had been trivial and easily remedied. Or the problem was so big it just couldn't be fixed. Unfortunately for Ruby, it was the latter. She'd thrown a clot into her mesenteric vasculature, infarcting her entire bowel. Toxins were flooding her system. She was dying and there was nothing anyone could do.

To say they were all shocked was an understatement. The nine-year-old had survived a horrific car smash but had been expected to make a full recovery from her head injury. Unfortunately, her conscious level had masked what was going on in her belly and she wasn't expected to see out the day.

Maggie sat in with Nash and the surgeon and the social worker as they broke the news to Ruby's family. Their reaction was heart-wrenching and Maggie blinked rapidly to clear the mist of tears from her eyes as the family broke down. Whatever sadness she felt was insignificant to what the family were experiencing, and they needed her to be strong and do her job.

They limped through the next couple of hours, getting Ruby out of bed for cuddles with her parents—no easy feat still ventilated with all the associated tubes—and just trying to be there for the distraught family. When the first day-shift person arrived Maggie almost kissed their feet.

All the staff on the night shift were affected by what was going on in bed eight and there wasn't one of them that didn't want to go home to hug their kids or their loved ones and escape the unfolding tragedy.

It was well after eight by the time Maggie

finished handing over and catching up on her charting. She was tired but edgy and the prospect of going home to an empty house with no distractions from the image of Ruby stubbornly implanted in her head was depressing as hell. She knew she wasn't going to sleep, even though her body craved respite.

She got into the lift, too tired to take the stairs. It dinged open on the top floor and she headed for the fire exit that led out to the rooftop car park. Nash was halfway through it when she rounded the corner.

They looked at each other for a few moments, both a little battered from the long night with no rest stops and the emotional whammy of Ruby. 'Here you are,' he said. 'I went looking for you.'

'Here I am,' she said.

Nash stepped out into the car park and she followed him. The early sunshine had been usurped by heavy clouds and a cool breeze blew across the rooftop. It looked bleak, matching their mood perfectly. He turned back and opened his mouth to tell her how sorry he was about Ruby but she spoke first.

'Do you want to come back to my place?'

Nash blinked. He understood where the request was coming from. He'd seen how gutted she'd been when the surgeons had imparted their tragic news. Had felt it cut deep into his soul too, remembering Tammy. 'I thought we were a one-night-only deal,' he asked cautiously.

Maggie looked him straight in the eye, knowing it was wrong to want it. Want him. Like this. After tonight. But it was the only thing that made any sense right now—she wasn't going to question it. 'I don't want to be alone today.'

Her honesty hit him square in the solar plexus. Neither did he. He couldn't think of a better way to try and forget last night than being in Maggie's bed. 'Your car or mine?'

He drove and they sat in silence all the way to her place for which she was grateful. She didn't want to rehash or speculate about what would happen on the unit today. She wanted a shower and she wanted him. To get lost in him, to be wrapped up in him.

Nash followed her up the front steps as he had the other night and waited for her to open the door. She pushed it open and shut it again after them. She looked so desolate he wanted to make it better.

'You know Ruby's—'

Maggie held up her hand to silence him. 'Can we please just not talk?'

Nash nodded. She turned and he followed her through the house, into her bedroom and beyond to her en suite. She started peeling off her clothes and he joined her. When she was naked she flicked on the shower and stepped under the spray, holding out her arms to him.

He stepped in and she kissed him again and again, twining her arms around his neck, fusing her body with his. Kisses that took over, that made her forget. Deep and wet. Full of passion. Tinged with sorrow. She gave herself up to desire, letting it rise up and sweep the sadness away.

He soaped her body with long slippery strokes

and it was only when he was buried deep inside her, her legs wrapped around his waist, screaming his name as their climaxes hit, that she finally let go of the emotions that had threatened to rise up all morning.

She clung to his shoulders, her head buried in his neck as deep sobs shook her chest and her orgasm shook her to the core. When she spiralled down, she was more exhausted than she'd ever thought possible.

Nash turned off the taps, wrapped her in a fluffy towel, picked her up and carried her to the unmade bed. He lowered her to the sheets, joining her, spooning behind her, her head tucked under his chin, his arm clasped around her waist.

They were both asleep in minutes.

CHAPTER FIVE

NASH WOKE IN the darkened room to the patter of rain on the roof and Maggie on her side, her bare back to him, murmuring into the phone. He looked at his watch. Two o'clock. They'd been asleep for five hours.

He heard Maggie say, 'Just ringing to check on Ruby,' and 'I see,' and 'I'm fine,' before she hung up the phone. He reached out and laid his hand against her back between her shoulder blades and admired the contrast between his bronzed skin and the creamy richness of hers.

'Has she gone?'

Maggie nodded, her heart unbearably heavy. She didn't turn. 'An hour ago.'

The inevitability of Ruby's situation didn't ease

the impact of her words. Nash felt the little girl's death deep in his soul. Remembered Tammy's death and the devastating time that had followed all over again. He ran his hand across to Maggie's shoulder and gave it a gentle squeeze.

She shut her eyes at his comforting gesture, grateful for his silence. He'd known just what she'd needed like only another who worked in the field could. Her ex, an engineer, had never understood. He'd tried to fill her sadness up with clichéd phrases or contrived distractions, but none of them had worked as well as Nash's simple touch.

She didn't blame Peter. He'd tried hard but ultimately he hadn't been able to understand that every death took a little piece out of her soul. That she was diminished a little each time. That life made a little less sense with each tragedy.

'I'm sorry. I get too involved,' she murmured, falling back against her pillow and staring at the ceiling.

Nash rolled up on his elbow and looked into her sad brown eyes. He'd hoped that the nurses who had looked after Tammy at the end had been even half as involved. 'You should never apologise for that.'

Maggie smiled at him and lifted her palm to cradle his jaw, scratchy with blond stubble. 'Thank you.'

Nash turned his head and pressed a kiss to her palm. 'Are you hungry?'

His lips tickled against her palm and she moved it up higher, pushing her fingers into his thick, wavy hair. 'Starving.'

He kissed her briefly on the mouth. 'Stay there, I'll rustle us up something to eat.

'There's not much there, I'm afraid.' Maggie had been on a run of days before her nights and hadn't had the chance or the inclination to shop.

Nash rolled off the bed and grinned down at her. 'I am a master of making meals out of nothing.'

'Oh?' Maggie said, her gaze wandering down his naked body because he was just too magnificent to ignore.

He could feel his body respond to her blatant

enjoyment. 'Years of sharing flats and camping out back home have honed my culinary skills. Trust me.'

'Hmm,' she said, distracted by his burgeoning interest being displayed in full-frontal colour.

'Of course, if you keep looking at me like that, I'm just going to skip it and go straight to dessert.'

Maggie dragged her eyes away from his groin and blushed at the way his gaze was devouring her breasts. Her nipples hardened. But then her stomach growled into the silence and he chuckled.

'I'll be right back. Don't move a muscle.'

Nash made a brief detour into the bathroom for his underwear before heading for the kitchen. He opened the fridge and surveyed the sparse contents. A tub of yoghurt, skimmed milk, half a loaf of bread, a dried-out-looking carrot and three tomatoes.

Hmm. This was going to be a challenge even for him.

He opened the freezer and smiled. Maybe not.

'Dessert after all,' Nash said a few minutes

later, carrying in a tray with two bowls piled with ice cream.

'What—no loaves-and-fishes miracle today?' Maggie teased.

Nash laughed as he placed the tray on the bed. 'Please. Mother Hubbard has more food than you. But,' he said, 'I can't fault your taste in ice cream.'

A waft of something floral tickled her nose and Maggie's gaze fell to the other object on the tray. The miniature crystal vase she kept on her window sill was sporting a spray of frangipani blossoms. She glanced at Nash. 'They from my garden?'

He nodded. 'I hope you don't mind. I noticed them through the window.'

Maggie was inordinately touched. She hadn't pictured Nash as the romantic type but after the horror of last night it was the perfect gesture. She fingered a velvety petal admiring the vibrant yellow centre. 'Of course not. It was a lovely thought.'

He smiled at her and passed her a bowl. 'Eat up.'

Maggie sat and they ate the decadent chocolate macadamia ice cream in silence for a few moments. She felt tired but his company and the aroma of frangipani was keeping the dreadful sadness at bay.

Nash was distracted from the sensational taste by the swing of her breasts in his peripheral vision as she sat cross-legged and oblivious. Thoughts of dropping a spoonful of the dark ice cream on the centre of her chest and watching as her body heat warmed it and it ran in rivulets over her breasts taunted him.

He didn't think he would ever be able to get enough of seeing her naked. Maggie, he realised, was becoming addictive. Like double chocolate macadamia ice cream. Like a drug. 'Why don't we keep this thing going?' he asked casually as he took another mouthful.

Maggie paused with the spoon halfway to her mouth. Her heart skipped a beat. 'What thing?'

Nash swallowed. 'This,' he said, waving his empty spoon between them. 'Us.'

He watched her, waiting for her reaction. She piled some more ice cream on her spoon and popped it in her mouth.

'I know it was supposed to be a one-night deal, Maggie.' It was suddenly vitally important that he convince her. He couldn't think of another person he'd rather spend time with before he went overseas. 'But we've already stepped over that line. What harm can there be just having fun together for the next couple of months?'

What harm indeed? He made it sound so simple. So tempting. And maybe it was. Looking at him, at all his incredible male vitality, his youth, his vigour, the prospect of a relationship with him seemed utterly ludicrous. But sitting next to him eating ice cream, his bare broad shoulders so close she could lean in and press a kiss to them, a short affair involving mutual gratification seemed infinitely possible.

But. Was it right? It might seem lame to a lot of people but Maggie prided herself on always trying to do the right thing. Was having sex with a man ten years her junior the right thing to do? Just because they desired each other? And what about the gossip? Did she want to be the laughing stock of the hospital? The resident cradle-snatcher? 'I'm not really into casual.'

Nash chuckled. 'What's wrong with casual, Maggie May?'

His laugh was full of humour and sin and licked flames deep inside her, and she suddenly felt old. The differences between them were stark. He didn't have a problem with keeping it light, casual. Whereas she'd reached a stage in her life that craved the security of a relationship. Of waking up together everyday with someone. Maggie knew from experience how good it could be, how fulfilling. It wasn't that she was out there actively looking for it but she knew she was too old to play games.

After her divorce she hadn't thought she'd ever feel like this again, and she was surprised to discover she did now that Nash had forced her hand. She didn't want to invest too much emotional energy in someone who wasn't sticking around. Who wasn't a keeper. Because, as she'd already told him, she got too involved.

Nash was still trying out all the rides in the playground. And that was fine. But he could keep the swings and roundabouts. 'Nothing, I guess,' she murmured. 'Just not my style.'

'You have a style?'

Maggie smiled. 'I do now.' She finished her dessert and pushed the bowl onto the bedside table, easing herself down until she was on her back again, the pillow behind her head, the sheet pulled up.

'So we just stay…?'

Maggie wasn't quite sure how to define it. 'Friends?'

Nash eased back too, rolling on his side, propped on one elbow, while his other hand held the bowl. 'With benefits?'

God, he was beautiful, looking at her with the promise of an unrivalled sexual adventure. It sucked all the air from her lungs. Could she really pass that up? 'Maybe. Occasionally. I don't know.'

It wasn't much of a concession but he grinned at her. He was so addicted to Maggie he'd take whatever crumb she threw him at the moment. And then he'd make her so crazed with passion she'd be begging him to take up residence in her bed. Until January anyway. 'Maybe I could help to persuade you,' he murmured.

He placed the nearly empty bowl on the bed and slowly pulled the sheet away. He watched her watching him, desire making her eyes glazed and fluttering her eyelids to half-mast. He scooped his spoon into the bowl and filled it with soft ice cream. She was still watching him with those slumberous eyes and Nash felt a fist turn in his groin.

'I've been wanting to do this for ages,' he murmured as he held the spoon above her chest and watched the cold, gooey ice cream slide off and land dead centre. It practically sizzled.

Maggie gasped. 'That's freezing.'

Nash smiled as her nipples turned to engorged dusky icicles before his eyes. 'Not for long.' Already a brown puddle was gathering at the base of the cold glob.

'I hate being cold.'

But Nash could hear the desire trembling in her voice and watched as she stared at the melting ice cream, her bottom lip caught between her teeth.

'Are you just going to leave it there?' she demanded in a voice husky with need.

He dropped his head and kissed a creamy shoulder. 'Until it melts, and then I'm going to lick it all off.'

A rivulet escaped then and slowly trekked down the slope of her left breast. It was like warmed mud found in expensive spas and Nash watched its torturously slow trip, salivating. Finally it pooled at the base of her puckered nipple.

He grinned at her then dropped his head again to suck the melted ice cream from her nipple. He groaned as Maggie arched her back, forcing the sweet, hard, elongated contours deeper into his mouth. When he'd removed the chocolate coating he shifted slightly, trailing the flat of his tongue back up the muddy pathway that had traversed her breast.

Nash lifted his head, satisfied he'd lapped up every last bit, only to find tributaries of warmed chocolate oozing everywhere now. Over both breasts, towards her neck and down her ribcage like a sweet sticky web.

He looked up at her face. She had her eyes shut, her mouth open, panting softly, her hands fisted into the sheets. 'Now, this is the only way to eat ice cream,' he murmured.

Maggie was seeing stars behind her closed lids as the cool trickle felt like hundreds of fingers caressing her skin. His tongue searing, like a brand. Her hands were clenched, her toes curled. 'Don't stop,' she urged.

'Oh, honey,' he said, his lips against her nipple, pausing for a moment to lave it with more attention, enthralled by her whimper of ecstasy. 'I have no intention of stopping.'

And he proceeded to use his tongue all over, devouring every sweet sticky morsel. And when he was done with that, he went lower.

A month passed. Their relationship blossomed. Slowly at first, as Maggie tried to ration their time together, resisting the strong attraction that tugged at her continuously. But as they worked together more and more, their shifts coinciding more and more, walking to the car park together at the end of the shift, it seemed only natural to go back to her place together.

Still, it was clandestine. Maggie had some pride. She wasn't stupid, she knew it was no love match and had no desire for all and sundry to know. When he left she didn't want to face a barrage of *poor-Maggie* faces or sympathetic *how are yous?*

So they never went to dinner or the movies or anything that resembled a proper date. And that was fine by her. This was an affair—pure and simple. And both of them wanted the same thing—as much naked time as possible.

She wasn't interested in getting to know him. She didn't want to know about his dead sister, or his home, or his parents, or his grandmother, who he mentioned sometimes with such great affection. Or his plans for his flying paediatrician service. What was the point when he was leaving?

They'd go back to her place and steam up the bedroom windows well into the night, or day, depending on their shifts, and then do it all again the next time. As far as Maggie was concerned, the less she knew, the easier it would be when he got on that flight to London. Because one thing was for certain, she was going to miss the physical side of their relationship fiercely.

Waking up to his wandering hands, the feel of him deep inside her, the magic of his kiss. After being asexual for so long, he'd awoken a raging nymph that was going to be hard enough to deny. She didn't want to miss the non-physical aspect of Nash as well.

The first day in December dawned bright and early as Maggie watched it through the windows at work. The sunrise was glorious but she knew pretty soon she'd have to twist the knob and shut the blinds as the rays would be poking their intense fingers between the slats, stabbing the dilated pupils of her nocturnal staff with laser-like intensity.

Night duty, hideous at the best of times, was worse in summer. In winter, when the sun finally made an appearance it was a sign the shift was almost over and it had an instant reviving affect, like a magic wand. In summer the big yellow ball made an appearance at four a.m. with hours to go until knock-off time. In summer it sat low in the sky, mocking them all.

'Are you going to help me with this tree or what?'

Maggie sighed and shut the blinds, blocking out the depressingly early sunshine. God, she hated this hour of the morning. Between four and six was the hardest. It was the time when things most often went wrong. When the hours dragged the most. When she felt cold and hungry and even occasionally downright nauseous.

A Christmas tree was a great distraction from four-in-the-morning misery. 'Yep,' she said. 'Let's do it.'

She passed Nash at the central station hunched over his computer. He was rubbing at his jaw, looking haggard and tired and eminently sexy. He winked at her as she went by and her stomach did its wild jig thing. Not a good combination in its already delicate state.

Luckily the unit was quiet tonight, only three patients. That could all change in a matter of hours so it was nice to have lulls, no matter how brief, when they had time for frivolous things like Christmas decorations.

From where the tree was set up she could see all their patients. Bed three was still occupied by Toby, whose condition had continued to worsen. He was now on high-frequency ventilation and nitric-oxide therapy. The duff-duff noise of his ventilator reverberated through the unit like a stereo system as the pistoning membrane delivered a couple hundred breaths per minute.

His kidneys had also started to fail and a dialysis machine whirred quietly in complete contrast to the ventilator. It efficiently extracted, cleaned and returned Toby's blood via the vascath in his groin. Things were looking grim for the little boy and Maggie's gaze moved away quickly. She was unable to bear thinking about the battle he was waging to survive.

In bed four was a five-year-old girl who'd been bitten by a brown snake twelve hours previously and was on the unit for monitoring after administration of the antivenin. She was doing well, self-ventilating on room air and showing no signs of envenomation.

In bed eight was a four-week-old baby boy who'd had a tracheostomy for a critical airway a few days before. He'd been born with a rat's-tail trachea, interfering with his ability to breathe properly. He was coping well with his operation but needed to stay on the unit for a week to ten days for one-on-one management in the initial post-op stage.

Bed eight had seen six patients since Ruby's death a month ago but still the tragedy lingered in Maggie's soul. Some kids, some cases touched you more than others and made her wonder what the hell she was doing here. Luckily the patients since Ruby had all been in and out reasonably quickly helping to restore her faith.

Linda had put a Christmas CD on as they worked and it chimed happy, snowy, merry tunes and Maggie concentrated on them instead. It even managed to partially drown out the duff-duff noise of Toby's oscillator.

Maggie yawned, bone tired as she threw some tinsel around the base to cover up the rather utilitarian plastic bucket the tree was propped in. The vague queasy sensation she'd quelled earlier returned with a vengeance.

God—night duty sucked!

'Don't yawn,' Linda griped. 'It's contagious.'

'Sorry.' Maggie grimaced. 'I know I say this every night duty at this time, but I don't think I've ever felt so tired.'

Linda frowned at her. 'You burning the candle at both ends? You're always tired lately.'

Maggie busied herself in the box, scrabbling for more decorations. 'It's nights,' she dismissed casually. She wondered if Linda would be shocked to know who'd she'd been burning the candle with.

'No. It's daytime too,' Linda insisted.

Maggie blushed then and was pleased to still have her head in the box. She hadn't been getting much sleep the last month. Maybe a few hours a night—if that.

'Just getting old,' she joked.

'Hey, forty is not old,' Linda protested. 'It's the new thirty. Besides, you're only as old as you feel, or the man that you're feeling anyway.' Linda laughed raucously at her own joke.

Maggie flicked her gaze to Nash and caught him as he sneaked a glance her way, a grin on his face. 'Come on,' she said, deftly changing the subject. 'Let's use all this leftover tinsel to decorate each bed space. We can string it along the curtain rails.'

An hour later the unit was looking very Christmassy. Red and silver tinsel was entwined and looped through the curtain rails as well as along the desks of the central station and down the corridor. Colourful 'Merry Christmas' banners were stuck up on the windows at each bed space and the Christmas cards the unit had already started to receive were displayed on the main swing doors.

'I love Christmas,' Maggie sighed as she and Linda stood back to admire their handiwork.

'Not bad for a couple of hours' work,' Linda agreed. 'What do you reckon, Nash?'

Nash looked around at the transformed clinical environment. 'I think you two could get jobs as elves,' he said, and tried really hard not to think about Maggie in a tiny elf costume. And failed.

'You got your tree up yet, Maggie?' Linda asked.

'Nah. Not much point with just me.'

Nash saw the wistful look in her eyes as her gaze roamed around the room, reflecting the twinkling tinsel. She sounded a little sad and he suppressed the urge to stand and draw her into his arms.

'We had ours up two weeks ago. The kids' nagging was driving me insane,' Linda said with a laugh.

Maggie's gaze briefly settled on Nash's and he gave her one of his public smiles where his face said one thing but his tropical-island eyes said something much more intimate. She looked away, not wanting him to see the stupid jealousy that had seized her thinking about Linda and the six kids she was going to spoil rotten Christmas morning.

The yearning never went away. She could work and work and bury it deep but someone talking about their kids or a mother pushing a pram in a street and it all came crashing back.

'Well, I'm going to get something to eat before I throw up,' she announced, the horrible nausea persisting. *Would this night never end?*

'I'll join you,' Linda volunteered.

Waiting in the kitchen for the toast to pop was torturous. It smelled amazing as only toast could do to a stomach under revolt. Maggie placed her hand on her belly. 'Ugh. I think I really am going to throw up.'

As often as she felt like this on night shift, she'd never actually vomited.

Linda frowned at Maggie's pale face. 'Well, if I didn't know all about your fertility problems I'd ask the obvious question. Tired. Nauseous. You haven't skipped a period, have you?'

A surge of laughter bubbled up her throat. 'Don't be ridiculous.'

Linda quirked an eyebrow. 'Have you?'

Maggie stared at her colleague like she'd just grown horns. 'You can't be serious?'

'Sure.' She shrugged. 'Why not?'

'Because,' Maggie spluttered. It was preposterous. Totally preposterous. But the ruptured condom was suddenly all she could think about. Her fatigue vaporised. She squinted as she searched her memory for her last period.

'You are late,' Linda the Shrewd piped up.

'I'm forty,' Maggie dismissed, desperately trying to quell the stupid flutter of hope that had taken up residence in her heart. The toast popped and she removed it and started buttering it automatically. 'My period's been a bit all over the shop the last six months or so. Probably just menopausal.'

Linda looked at her dubiously. 'If you say so.'

Maggie nodded and was pleased when Linda let it drop. Because she couldn't. For the remaining hour of the shift it was there. Taunting her. Mocking her. A baby. A baby. A baby. And it didn't matter how many times she disregarded it and told herself to stop being foolish, she was infertile—*infertile, for God's sake*—it wouldn't quit.

A baby. A baby. A baby.

It whispered its promise to her insidiously. Glowing like a candle in the darkness. Shining like a beacon of hope. Which was crazy. *Beyond crazy.* She'd been diagnosed with idiopathic infertility in the prime of her life. How on earth could she conceive at all, never mind in the dying days of her dysfunctional fertility cycle? It didn't make any sense.

But she knew as she grabbed her bag from her locker that she was going to stop by the chemist's and buy a pregnancy test. Not because she believed it but because she didn't. Couldn't. A simple test would tell her the inevitable in two minutes and then she could stop all these ridiculous thoughts and get some sleep.

'Maggie.'

Maggie stopped short as Nash greeted her in the corridor outside the staff change rooms.

Nash.

Oh, no. Among the malestrom of thoughts in her head she hadn't even considered Nash.

Nash checked behind him, making sure no one was within earshot. 'I have something to do after I knock off so I won't be around till about ten.'

Maggie, still dazed, her mind racing, didn't notice the vagueness of his statement. 'Oh, okay, sure.' That was good. It would give her time to get the ridiculous test out of the way, quash the insane thoughts and have a couple of hours' sleep before he joined her.

He looked over his shoulder again. 'Do you want to give me your keys so you don't have to get out of bed to let me in?'

His voice had dropped a couple of notches and Maggie didn't even notice over the *baby, baby, baby* chant going on inside her head. 'Sure.' She rooted around in her handbag and handed him her spare set of house keys.

Nash frowned. Maggie, who had insisted on the secrecy, didn't seem too cagey about handing over her keys to him. She usually got cranky if he so much as smiled at her at work. 'Are you okay?'

Maggie's head shot up. 'Yes, why? I'm fine,' she babbled. 'Just fine.'

Nash chuckled. She looked tired but also wired and definitely a little spaced. She was almost delirious. Lord knew, he'd felt that way many a time after a long night. 'Drive carefully, Maggie May.' He knew she lived close but driving after night duty was a real hazard.

She gave Nash a tight smile, thinking about the

location of a chemist's that opened early. 'See you later.'

Nash frowned again at Maggie's back. Maggie May was a definite no-no at work. What the hell was wrong with her this morning?

Maggie felt sick just looking at the test as she pulled it out of the pack. Sick and nervous. But was it a positive result that was making her feel that way or a negative one? She put it on the kitchen bench. She'd been to the toilet before leaving work and doubted very much if she could produce any urine for the test right at this moment.

So she made a cup of tea, relying on the diuretic effect of it to work its magic on her bladder. She sat out on her back deck in the morning sunshine, the December sun already packing quite a punch. She tried to concentrate on her lovely gardens bordered with the native trees and shrubs she'd lovingly planted with her own hands, but her mind kept wandering to what colour she was going to paint the nursery and for a little while she let herself indulge in the fantasy.

When she finished her cup she went and poured another, torn between wanting to do the test and being terrified of the result. If it was negative, which of course it was going to be, she knew she was going to be bitterly disappointed. She shouldn't be. It was wrong to want it. It was a dream she'd given up on long ago but the yearning in every fibre of her being this morning was almost a physical ache.

God, she'd gone through a decade of this—negative pregnancy tests—waiting for that magic second line or the dot to turn blue or whatever newfangled gimmick the test boasted to relay the happy-sad news to its user. How could she go through it all again?

The second cup of tea disappeared and Maggie forced herself to stop being such a coward and just do it. She made her way to the much closer main bathroom, not trusting herself to walk the extra distance to her en suite without chickening out.

She followed the directions but when she held it in her hands straight afterwards she couldn't bear to look. She couldn't bear to see the little red sign in the window. Not again. She left it on the cistern, washed her hands in the bathroom and fled back out to the deck to muster some courage.

Nash had a smile on his face as big as Tasmania when he opened Maggie's door. He crept in with his booty, not wanting to wake her. Not yet anyway. Unlike him, she didn't have to work again tonight but he knew better than to disturb those first few catatonic hours of sleep after night duty.

He quietly placed the pre-decorated four-foot Christmas tree on her coffee table and plugged the lights into the nearest power point. They glowed in multicoloured splendour and he hoped Maggie was going to love it.

She'd looked so sad earlier that morning when she'd admitted to not bothering to decorate the house for Christmas because she lived alone that he'd resolved then and there to rectify the situa-

tion. Maybe that's why she'd been a little preoccupied? Maybe contemplating another lonely
Christmas had made her a little melancholy.

Well, not this year. *This year she had him and
he was going to make it a Christmas to remember.*

He smiled again, heading for the main
bathroom, not wanting to risk using her en suite.
He wondered how long she'd sleep for and
couldn't wait for her to wake up. Should they
make love first or should he drag her outside and
reap the rewards of her gratitude then?

He smiled as he zipped up and reached for the
flush button, noticing for the first time the
round plastic disc-shaped device sitting on the
cistern. Nash frowned as he reached for it. It
took a few more seconds for him to figure out
that he was indeed seeing what it was he
thought he was seeing.

The Christmas tree was instantly forgotten.

What the…?

He strode from the toilet, pregnancy test in
hand, and stalked into her bedroom. He could

feel a white-hot ball burning in his stomach like acid reflux. Not there. Where the hell was she? Her car was outside so she had to be home. His pulse galloped at his temples and reverberated through his head in great, angry crashes. His grip tightened on the test, feeling it creak as the plastic protested his grip. No wonder she'd been so screwy. How long had she suspected?

'Maggie?' he called as he stormed through the house. 'Maggie?'

Maggie, still trying to summon the nerve to go and look at the result, felt her heart stop as Nash's voice carried out to her.

She stood and turned to face the door as Nash stepped out onto the deck and she knew by his face it was already too late. And when he opened his mouth she could hear the barely contained menace.

'You want to tell me about this?'

CHAPTER SIX

MAGGIE WAS TOO shocked for a moment to do much of anything other than stare at his beautiful face, tense and shuttered for the first time since she'd known him.

Then her gaze flicked to the pregnancy test he was holding up and she saw a little pink sign and she was too stunned to speak.

'Well?' Nash demanded.

His voice cracked through her momentary paralysis. She reached for it, taking it from him, staring at the test window with the pretty pink plus sign.

Pregnant. Pregnant. *A baby. A baby. A baby.* Her hands shook. But how? It couldn't be. It had to be wrong.

'It's positive,' she said, looking at him for confirmation, feeling like a dyslexic toddler.

'I can see that,' he said grimly.

'But…how?' More with the two-year-old questions.

Nash's jaw tightened. 'I guess it was when the condom broke' Once. Damn it! Once! Every other time they'd used nice, new, never-fail condoms.

Maggie knew he was opening his mouth, could hear him speaking, but none of his words made sense. Didn't he remember she was infertile? 'No. I mean… How…? I can't… I'm not supposed to be able to fall pregnant.'

Nash took the test off her and held it up. 'Wrong.'

Maggie knew on a visceral level that Nash was not happy. Knew he had every right to be angry, but wrapping her head around this was taking some time. And despite it all her insides were singing. *Yes, singing.*

A baby. A baby. A baby.

'Where are you going?' Nash growled as Maggie pushed past him, scurrying into the house.

'I'm taking the other test.'

Nash stared after her. What the hell? He went after her, finding her rooting through her handbag in the kitchen. 'The other test?'

'They didn't have any single test kits,' she said, locating the other pink box and heading for the toilet.

'There's no point,' he said, following her. 'it'll be the same.'

Maggie turned around. 'It's wrong. It has to be.' She was trying not to get excited. Trying not to get carried away. How many tests had she done in the past convinced she was pregnant? How many times had her hopes been raised, only to be dashed so wretchedly?

Nash sighed, resignation already taking a firm foothold in the mountain of his blind panic. 'It's not. You don't get false positives. Only false negatives.'

If he'd had any idea how much she wanted to cling to that, he would have kept his mouth firmly shut. But Maggie had been down this road one too many times. She was forty, for crying out loud. *And* infertile. 'It's wrong,' she insisted, before closing the door in his face.

Because if he was right, if the test was right, it would be just too surreal.

Nash paced outside, his brain churning, thoughts tossing around like garments in a tumble-dryer. He checked his watch. A minute later he checked it again. What the hell was taking her so long? 'Maggie.' He banged on the door. 'What on earth are you doing in there?' he growled. *How long did it take to wee on a stick?*

Maggie was startled. The flow she was trying to coax instantly disappeared. She couldn't believe her bladder was choosing this moment for an attack of performance anxiety. She could see the shadow of Nash's pacing footsteps in the polished floorboards under the crack of the door which was putting a little more pressure on her urinary tract.

'Give me a break,' she said crankily. 'I only did this twenty minutes ago. It's not a bottomless cup.'

'Do you want me to turn a tap on?'

Maggie glared at the door. 'I want you to go away.'

'I'm not going anywhere.'

Great! Maggie shut her eyes and concentrated. Hard. On waterfalls and pouring rain and dripping taps. And warm, yellowish fluid of another origin. Surrounding her baby. Nourishing it. Cocooning it. Protecting it. Rocking it to sleep. She smiled at the thought and finally found the release she was after.

This time she looked straight away, preparing to count to one hundred and twenty Mississippis before she saw a change in the test window. But it was there already. A result. Another pink plus sign.

Maggie stood for a few seconds, just staring at it, until another bang on the door interrupted the sheer incredulity she was feeling.

'Damn it, Maggie.'

Maggie opened the door. Nash was looking equal parts harried and annoyed. And when he quirked his eyebrow at her she said, 'I'm pregnant,' and promptly burst into tears.

Nash stood temporarily paralysed as Maggie's face crumpled and great heaving sobs screwed her face into one only a mother could love. *Oh, God. Not tears.* How could he be angry with her when she was so heartbroken? Still, he was surprised at her reaction. For a woman who'd spent a good part of an entire decade and a lot of hard-earned money trying to get pregnant, he'd thought she'd be ecstatic.

Maybe this news was as appalling to her as it was him? Maybe she'd got past the urge to procreate? The thought was comforting and he took her in his arms and held her while she sobbed into his chest. 'Shh,' he crooned, stroking her hair. 'It's okay.'

Maggie clung to his shirt while the news swirled around her in a whirlpool of emotions. Excitement. Incredulity. Amazement. Disbelief. But mostly joy. She was delirious with joy. After years of yearning, years of desperate maternal cravings she was finally going to be a mother.

'This doesn't have to be the end of the world,' Nash murmured against her forehead. 'We have options. It all might be a bit of a mess right now but we'll figure it out.'

A bit of a mess? Maggie pulled away from his chest and looked at him. What on earth was he talking about? Things were perfect. 'Are you kidding?' she sniffled, wiping the heels of her hands across her cheekbones. 'This is the best thing that has ever happened to me. Ever.'

Nash frowned. Her face was blotchy, her nose was red but she was suddenly smiling at him like a crazy person. 'So…those were tears of happiness?'

Maggie nodded. 'Supreme happiness.'

'Right,' he said, hoping he didn't look as confused as he felt. He'd forgotten how contrary women could be.

'I need another cup of tea. Do you want one?' she asked, brushing past him, her mind on nursery colours and baby names.

Cup of tea? Nash watched her disappearing

back. A slug of whiskey would be better. *Much better.* He took a few moments to let the enormity of it all sink in. A father. He was going to be a dad. A memory of his father's face at his sister's funeral rose through the jumble of his thoughts, the misery and desolation etched deeply into the grooves of his forehead, grooves that had never gone away. He drew in a ragged breath, fighting against the tonne of bricks sitting on his chest.

Maggie was humming—*humming, for God's sake*—when he joined her in the kitchen. She handed him his mug as she headed for the deck.

Maggie placed her cup on the wooden tabletop outdoors but she didn't sit. She couldn't. She felt like a kid on Christmas Eve, excitement and nervous energy making sitting still an impossibility. She hugged herself as she stared at her small back yard, picturing a fort in one corner—with a ladder and a slippery dip. And a set of swings in the other.

Nash watched her, staring aimlessly. Where the hell did they go from here? 'So?'

Nash's voice intruded in on her little fantasy and Maggie turned to face him. For the first time she noticed his pallor. He usually looked so tanned, it was odd seeing the colour leached from his handsome face. And everything about him betrayed a tense watchfulness, from the tightness around his mouth to the erectness of his stance.

He always looked so loose, so relaxed, like he was about to break out into the broadest grin. But not right now. Right now he looked like any number of parents she'd been involved with who'd just been given bad news. He looked like he'd had the stuffing knocked out of him.

'Oh, Nash, I'm sorry. I know you never wanted this.'

Nash nodded and felt the tension in his shoulders ease a little. Maggie had at least acknowledged that this news affected both of them. He pulled out a chair and sat down. She followed suit. 'What do you want to do now?'

Maggie spread her hands. 'I honestly haven't thought about it.' She looked into his face and saw worry etching lines into his forehead and around his eyes.

'But look,' she assured him, placing her palms flat on the table, 'you don't have to worry. I don't want anything from you. I understand. It's okay. I'm going to be fine. We're going to be fine.'

She felt a pang in her chest but it got lost amidst the marvel of being a *we*. She and the baby.

She was a we.

Nash frowned. 'Don't be ridiculous, Maggie. This baby is my responsibility too and I don't shirk my responsibilities,' he snapped.

Maggie gaped at him, stunned by his categorical rejection of her offer to absolve him of consequence. The man looked like he'd fly all the way to London today if he could, even if it meant he had to flap his own arms.

Maggie gave a half-laugh. Did he mean he wanted to be an *us?* 'What?'

'You heard me,' he said tersely.

'But…but why? This isn't the Victorian age, Nash. Women can and do have babies without a man to take care of them. You have a whole career planned. You really don't have to worry about this.'

Nash, feeling rather contrary himself amidst the roller-coaster of emotions he was experiencing, suddenly felt kind of disposed of. 'Were you even going to tell me?'

Maggie shook her head dazedly, spun out by the unexpected turn of events. 'What?'

'If I hadn't walked in here today and discovered the test, would you have told me?'

She struggled with the question. 'Yes. No. I…don't know… Maybe?'

Nash shot her a hard look. 'Maybe? Well, that's just great, Maggie.'

'Oh, come on, Nash,' Maggie pleaded, chilled by the way the warmth in his tropical island eyes had turned glacial. 'I've only just found out. I haven't really thought anything through.'

One blond eyebrow shot up. 'Maybe?' he repeated.

'You leave for the other side of the world in a

month. Wouldn't it be wrong of me to dump this in your lap now? What possible good could come of it? You have this whole plan for your future. London for a few years and then setting up the flying paediatrician service. A baby doesn't figure into that. Anyway, you don't want to be a father. You told me that yourself.'

'Not wanting to have children when there are none is entirely different from finding out someone's carrying your baby and it's very much a reality.'

'I didn't plan this, Nash.' Hell, she'd have never thought it possible!

He sighed. 'I know.'

'Well, what do you want, then?' Maggie's heart thundered at the possibility that Nash might want to be part of his baby's life. Part of her life. Was that what he wanted? What she wanted?

She had a sudden flash of him with Brodie on his hip that day in the Radio Giggle studio and the way he'd been with Dougy. He was great with kids.

Nash stood and raked his hand through his hair.

'Damn it, Maggie, I don't know. This is a lot to process.'

For him, maybe. For her it felt like she'd finally arrived at her destination. She was already this baby's mother, already loved it more than she had words to describe.

'I mean, do you even want me to be a part of this baby's life?' he demanded.

She shrugged. 'I…I suppose…'

'Gee, Maggie. Could you be a little more enthusiastic?'

'I'm sorry, I didn't mean that to sound half-hearted. I'm just surprised that you do, that's all. I wouldn't have thought for a minute that you would.'

Nash clenched his jaw at her unintended insult. He was from the country, where men were honourable and took their obligations seriously.

'It's my responsibility, Maggie. I told you that. I like to think I'm an honourable man and honourable men do not walk away from their mistakes.'

Even as the word came out Nash wished he could retract it. He saw Maggie freeze and felt like the worse kind of bastard. 'I'm sorry, I didn't mean…'

Maggie sat very still. He saw their baby as some kind of error? A blunder? A slip-up? She placed her hand across her stomach as if she could protect the baby from Nash's words. No matter what happened, she would never look upon this occurrence as a mistake. The fact that he did spoke volumes. 'Oh, I think you did.'

Nash pushed the pads of his fingers into his shut eyes and then dropped his hands to his sides. God, he felt tired. 'I'm sorry, that came out all wrong.'

'Really? Maybe it was a Freudian slip.'

'Hell, Maggie, it was the wrong choice of word from the depths of fuzzy night-duty brain. Don't read any more into it than that.'

Except sometimes when people were tired and their guards were down, they said exactly what they were thinking. Their filters didn't work and their real thoughts spewed out.

Maggie felt her ire rising. She didn't want to

be anyone's responsibility or her baby to be anyone's mistake. She glared at him. 'We're not going to be your cross to bear, Nash.'

Nash rolled his eyes at her melodrama. 'Oh, please. I just need some time to think about it. Figure it out.'

Maggie felt more and more like an inconvenience. A problem to be solved. A puzzle to crack. Okay, yes, he was tired and this was a shock. But she sure as hell wasn't going to hang around waiting for *him* to figure *her* out, figure their *mistake* out.

She stood. 'Well, why don't you go and do that? You know your way out,' she said frostily.

Nash looked at her as she regarded him with utter disdain. She was angry and he wasn't exactly in the best of moods. He thought about how happy he'd been when he'd opened the front door half an hour ago and couldn't believe so much could change so quickly.

One thing was for sure, this conversation needed a clear head and open mind and Maggie looked more unreachable than she had in the beginning when she'd refused to even give them a chance. *Damn it!*

'Fine,' he said tersely. 'We'll talk later.' And he turned on his heel, not stopping to look back as he strode through the house and let himself out the front door.

Maggie heard the bang from the deck and dragged in a gulp of air, her hands shaking. That had gone well.

Not.

She picked up their mugs, made her way back into the kitchen and placed them in the sink, her mind completely preoccupied, seesawing between giddy delight and irritation at Nash's behaviour. But ultimately nothing could trump the realisation that she was pregnant—actually pregnant.

She was grinning as she detoured through the lounge-room to check that Nash had locked the door after his hasty exit. She stopped short in the archway as her gaze fell on the decorated Christmas tree that stood in one corner.

Despite the hour, the artfully spaced fairy-lights winked on and off and a small 'Oh,' escaped her lips involuntarily. It was beautiful. Rich and green with red tinsel, frosted white ornaments and a gorgeous golden star.

'Nash,' she whispered, her hand pressed to her heart, moved by his gesture.

It was typical Nash. To her surprise he'd proven to be quite the romantic. Their relationship may have been clandestine but it hadn't stopped him from constantly touching her heart with little surprises. From the vase of frangipani blossoms to candlelight picnics in bed and deliveries of her favourite chocolates. He really had spoiled her. But the tree was something else.

She sat on the lounge and watched the lights blink on and off, her anger at him dissolving temporarily, suddenly miserable that he had left as he had before she'd had a chance to thank him.

She'd deliberately not thought of Christmas in relation to him. She knew he was working on

Christmas Day, as was she, but she hadn't wanted to pry or push as to his plans for the night. She'd hoped they'd spend it together. But now? She was pretty sure whatever they had been building had just come tumbling down.

Nash went to work that night with a lot on his mind. He'd barely slept so he was more tired, crankier and grouchier than he'd ever been in his life. And everyone noticed. Because Nash was never any of those things. Not even in the midst of a crisis. He was laid-back, unfailingly cheerful and if it was there, usually found the humour in any situation.

But tonight he was tense, snappy and grim-faced. And the nurses avoided him like the plague. Lucky for them their quiet streak was continuing so contact with Nash could be minimised. The snake bite patient had gone to the ward at lunchtime, which left only Toby and the *duff, duff, duff* of his ventilator and the critical airway baby.

So the night was interminable. Too much time to

think. To dwell on things. A father. He was going to be a father! Something he'd made a conscious decision never to be. Something he'd never even imagined. Had always, in fact, taken every precaution to prevent. But it had happened anyway.

His mother would be ecstatic. So would his father. It wasn't enough that their grandchildren already numbered twelve, they doted on each and every one and were overjoyed that his sisters didn't appear to be finished yet.

But he didn't want that for himself. Not now. Not ever. And yet here he was. Why? And why with the one woman who was rapidly coming to mean more than just a three-month fling to him. She ticked every box—smart, fascinating, gorgeous, funny and great between the sheets. Things had been going so well. And now this.

Still his honour demanded that he do the right thing and by the time he pulled out of the rooftop car park the next morning he knew exactly what that involved.

* * *

Maggie was lying on the couch at around nine-thirty, absently staring at the blinking tree lights just visible in the daylight, her mind adrift, when a knock at the door sounded. She'd fallen asleep on the couch late last night, staring at the lights twinkling in the tinsel. She'd been watching some dreadful midnight movie but the kaleidoscope of colour kept drawing her gaze and eventually she'd switched the TV off and just lain back and watched.

She let her head loll off the edge of the lounge slightly and looked back through her fringe to the front door. She could see a large male silhouette and she didn't have to be a rocket scientist to figure out who was calling at this hour.

For a moment she contemplated ignoring it, feigning sleep, but whatever else had happened here yesterday, whatever challenges they faced right now, she needed to thank him for the tree.

A second knock spurred Maggie into a sitting position. A wave of nausea flooded her and she waited a moment for it to pass. 'Coming,' she called. She was dressed in her usual bed attire, a pair of men's silky boxers and a faded old singlet T that didn't quite meet the waistband.

She felt a fleeting sense of propriety but felt too rough around the edges to pay it much heed. Nash had seen her in a lot less. In fact, she doubted he'd ever seen her so covered up in a just-awaken state.

Maggie wasn't prepared when she opened the door for the impact of him. Had she forgotten in just twenty-four hours how he could reduce her to jelly? Even his bleak-looking face wasn't enough to dampen the roar of her hormones. Had she always felt like this or was it just the knowledge that part of him was growing inside her? A purely biological connection left over from primitive man?

'Hi.' Maggie grasped the doorknob like it was her anchor as his presence threatened to suck her into an alternate universe—prehistoric and littered with clubs and caves.

Nash curled his fingers into his palms to stop

from reaching for her. She looked so damn good, her sleepy eyes and tousled hair reminding him of myriad early morning wake-ups with her snuggled close, the intoxicating smell of her, of them, rousing him to instant alertness.

He wanted to erase the last twenty-four hours, haul her into his arms and drag her into bed, drag her under him, feel her tightness around him. He was shocked to realise he'd missed her.

'Can I come in?'

Maggie stood aside and he prowled past into the lounge room. His back was to her as he stood in front of the Christmas tree. 'I didn't get a chance to thank you yesterday…for the tree. It's…beautiful. I'm…touched.'

He concentrated on a yellow light blinking merrily, gilding the nearby red tinsel. He shrugged. 'It's Christmas. Everyone should have a tree.'

'Even if you live alone?'

He turned to face her. 'Especially if you live alone.'

Maggie's breath caught in her throat. He look

tired—desperately tired—and yet he managed somehow to cut right to what was important. How could he be so profound on such little sleep? And then a thought snaked through her brain, seductive in its joy—she was never going to spend another Christmas alone.

He turned to face her, holding up a brown paper bag. 'I bought Danish pastries.'

Maggie was new to this morning sickness thing but one thing she knew with absolute certainty was that her constitution was not up to handling anything so decadent.

'Let's eat on the deck,' she murmured.

Ten minutes later she could smell the eucalyptus and hear a kookaburra laughing in a distant tree. 'You look tired,' she said as he tucked into a flaky morsel.

Nash stopped in mid-chew. 'I didn't really sleep yesterday.'

Maggie sipped her tea. Neither had she. Between daydreaming about the baby and their argument replaying in her mind, sleep had been elusive. But at least she'd been able to recharge her batteries overnight. Poor Nash had had to stay awake, be alert, professional. 'Are we still quiet?'

Nash nodded. 'Just the two. There was a retrieval call though, just before I left—a fourteen-year-old riding a skateboard, suspected subdural.'

'No helmet?'

Nash shot her a tired smile. 'How'd you guess?'

Maggie didn't bother to answer the rhetorical question even to fill the weird silence. It was awkward between them now but no matter how much she yearned for their easy familiarity, she wouldn't have changed the course of events that had brought them to this moment for all the money in the world.

Nash swallowed the last of his pastry and licked his lips. He looked into her fudge-brownie eyes and drew in a steadying breath as his pulse hammered through his temples. 'I think you should come to London with me. Let's give this thing a go.'

Maggie's eyes widened and she almost

dropped her hot tea in her lap. 'What?' she spluttered. She'd known he had something he wanted
to say but this was totally out of left field.

'You said it yesterday. My career path is taking
me to London. It's something I've worked years
towards and a vital step in my plans for the flying
paediatrician service. I have to go. I want to go.
But I can't just take off when I have a responsibility to you. So come to London with me.'

Just like that? Pick up on a whim because she was
his responsibility and he was lumbered with her?
Because he thought they should *give it a go?* 'No.'

'Maggie.'

'No.'

'Come on, it's London,' he cajoled. 'It's magic.'

'I know,' she said frostily. 'I've lived there.
Back when you were in high school.' She suppressed the urge to say 'little boy.'

Nash groaned. 'Oh, Maggie, not the age
thing again.'

She shook her head. 'No. Not the age thing
again. But if you think I'm going to fly to

London and shack up with my toy boy who wants to *give it a go* just because I'm pregnant with his child, you're nuts.'

Nash winced. He hadn't meant it to sound like that. So…temporary. So ill-conceived. He hadn't meant that way at all. 'I'm sorry. I'm saying it all wrong.' He reached into his pocket and pulled out a blue velvet box and put it on the table. 'Marry me.'

This time, Maggie plonked her mug on the table for fear that she really was going to upend its contents in her lap. She stared at the box then at him, struck dumb for a few seconds. When she did find her voice it sounded all high and breathy.

'Did you just…propose to me?'

Nash frowned. He couldn't work out if she was happy or annoyed. Wasn't that what women wanted? A wedding band? That's what most women to date had wanted from him.

Okay, it hadn't been the most romantic of proposals but this wasn't any ordinary situation. This was never the way or the circumstances he'd ever pictured proposing under. Not that he'd ever pictured it. *Hell!*

He rubbed his forehead, blaming his tiredness. He hadn't planned on this when he'd knocked on her door that morning. 'Sorry, I know it wasn't exactly hearts and flowers.'

Maggie blinked. Now, that was the world's biggest understatement! Had he just asked her to marry him out of some warped sense of duty? She supposed she should be admiring his strong honourable streak—there weren't a lot of men like him around these days—but she was too stunned.

Maggie reached for some composure amidst her galloping thoughts and thrumming pulse, ignoring the lure of the little blue box. 'Do you love me, Nash?'

Her quiet question took him unawares. He'd thought for a moment she was going to explode and had been bracing himself for it when her calm enquiry hit him fair in the solar plexus.

The L word.

He'd avoided saying it to any woman all his

adult life. Not because he was afraid of it but because no one had ever claimed that sort of place in his heart and he'd always deplored men who bandied it about like it was some trivial emotion. What his parents had, his grandparents had was not remotely trivial.

And no one had even come close. Not even a little. Until Maggie. 'I like you. A lot. You're like no one I've ever met. I *love* what we have. I *love* being with you. I *love* waking up next to you.' It was as honest as he could be right now.

Maggie nodded slowly. Even if she hadn't been able to read the unspoken *but,* his stricken face gave it away.

But. I don't love you.

Her chest grew tighter and tighter and it took a moment to figure out she'd been holding her breath. *Oh, God!* She sucked in air, her gasping alveoli filling with a much-needed rush of oxygen as her brain staggered under the weight of her sudden realisation.

She loved him.

How? How had this happened? When? But even as she asked herself, she knew the answer. The day he'd decorated a serving tray with frangipani blossom from her garden because he'd known after an ugly night shift how much she'd needed to see a little beauty. And every little romantic gesture since that had made their time together so special.

How could she have spent all this time pretending that their relationship had been purely physical? That she could spend three months in his arms and be able to wave him off in January like nothing had ever happened. What a farce!

Even just looking at him now, with weariness etched into the furrows on his forehead and the crinkles around his eyes, she loved him so much she felt like she was going to burst with it.

She placed a hand on her belly, another realisation hitting home. She wasn't just carrying Nash's child. Not any more. She was pregnant by the man she loved. Their baby had been conceived out of love.

The desire to give way to full-blown panic

blossomed. But amidst the ringing bells and clanging clocks echoing in her head a part of her knew that to betray her inner turmoil would be stupid. That she loved him was immaterial, that she wanted what was in that box didn't matter, when he obviously didn't feel the same way.

'Look, Nash, I understand that you have strong feelings about responsibility and duty. I mean, you're fulfilling a childhood promise to your sister so I get it that you're a man of honour.' She paused, searching for the right words. 'But let's not compound this issue by doing something rash like marrying for all the wrong reasons. I already have one divorce to my name.'

She was proud of how calm she sounded. How rational. And she didn't miss the slight sag to Nash's shoulders either.

'I'm not going to shirk this,' Nash said.

Maggie shivered at the steel in his voice and wished with all her heart that his insistence came out of love instead of honour. She wasn't prepared to disrupt her life and pine away in a loveless partnership on the other side of the world with a man who'd only married her out of duty. But she knew she'd follow him to Antarctica if he just said the three magic words.

She shrugged. 'So send money.'

Nash stilled as she presented him with the perfect solution. Support Maggie and the baby financially here in Australia while fulfilling his own dreams on the other side of the world. But even as his head turned it over, his heart rejected it outright. Whether he liked it or not, he'd helped form a new life. And already he was thinking of it as flesh and blood instead of a contraception failure. As his baby. Didn't every child deserve to have two parents?

Okay, he might only be away for a couple of years but did he want to miss out on such a vital, formative time in his child's life? 'I want to teach my kid how to kick a ball.'

Despite her resolve, Maggie was assailed with images of Nash standing behind a little blue-eyed blond demonstrating the perfect technique with a footy.

And I want you to love me.

Maggie's heart knew there were just some things you couldn't have. 'Commute.'

Nash gave her an exasperated look. See his kid once every few months? No. 'Fine…' He rubbed his eyes as all his dreams, his promises, crumpled before him. 'I'll stay.'

Maggie shook her head vigorously. 'No. Oh, no,' she rejected vehemently. 'I'm not having you blame me, or the baby, in years to come because you didn't get your time at Great Ormond Street.'

Nash reached across the table and grasped her hands, brushing a thumb back and forth over the prominent veins in the back of her hand. 'So come with me. Let's see how things pan out.'

Maggie fought against the pull of him that she felt at a visceral level, in every pulse stroke, every cell. But where would she be if they didn't pan out? No. Maturity had its advantages and she'd be a fool to ignore her fundamental needs. That was for the young.

She wasn't prepared to go with him for anything less than love. The fact that he didn't love her, that he would never love her, twisted like a knife. She pulled her hands from his. 'No.'

Nash stared at her resolute gaze. 'So what now?'

She pushed the box towards him with one finger, like it was full of red-back spiders. She didn't want a duty ring from him. 'You go home to bed and we talk another time.'

Nash nodded. He didn't want to go home. He'd grown accustomed to sleeping with her and hated going back to his Maggie-less apartment.

He picked up the box, pocketed it and stood. 'Okay. But this isn't over, Maggie May.' He moved towards her and crouched beside her chair, placing his hand over hers, hands that seemed to almost permanently cradle her belly these days. He threaded his fingers through hers. 'Not by a long shot.'

And then he stood again and turned away, once

again leaving with things unresolved. But one thing he knew for sure—as messed up as it was, she was carrying his baby, *his baby,* and he would take care of his child.

CHAPTER SEVEN

IT WAS HARD getting out of bed at three a.m. under the best of circumstances and Maggie knew in a few short months she was going to have to get used to it, but when you were exhausted and morning sickness had kicked in with a vengeance, it was that much harder. But she was on retrieval call and a four-year-old child in Rockhampton with epiglottitis needed intensive care.

So she dragged herself out of bed, threw up in the toilet, brushed her teeth, donned some jeans and a T-shirt, pulled a comb through her hair and drove to the hospital.

'Hell, Maggie, you look awful!' Linda exclaimed as Maggie entered the unit.

'It's three in the morning,' she grouched. The

festive decorations failed to distract her precarious constitution or her mood.

Linda gave her a this-is-my-third-night-I-have-six-kids-and-I'm-almost-a-decade-older-than-you look but wisely commented no further about Maggie's early morning roughness. 'Nash is already here,' she announced.

Maggie almost threw up on the spot again. *Oh, God, not Nash.* Please, not Nash. 'Great,' she muttered under her breath as she walked to the retrieval room where all the equipment was stored.

Nash had already started loading what they needed into a large trolley, which would accompany them to the airport. His broad back was facing her and her gaze was automatically drawn to the way his retrieval shirt pulled across the width of his shoulders and how his Levi's lovingly hugged the contours of his butt.

A rush of love welled in her chest, stirring her nausea, and she took a deep, cleansing breath. 'Hi.'

Nash turned at the sound of her voice, the neutral greeting he'd been practising since he'd learned they'd be going out together tonight dying on his lips. It had been four days since he'd seen her and she looked like hell. He took a step towards her. 'Are you okay?'

Maggie gave him an exasperated look. 'It's three a.m.,' she said, wishing she'd taken the time to slap on some make-up.

Couldn't a girl look a little rough around the edges after a rude early morning wakening? How the hell he managed to look so good she'd never know. Her heart was doing a crazy love-sick dance just looking at him.

Nash's heart thudded in his chest. He'd seen her early in the morning both at work and at play so he knew it wasn't that. 'Is everything okay with…the baby?'

Maggie glared at him, taking a quick look behind her to see if anyone had overheard. 'Baby's doing just fine,' she said tersely.

She, on the other hand, was not. Another wave of nausea hit her and Maggie prayed for a smooth flight.

'Maybe Linda should call someone else in?' Nash suggested.

'There isn't anyone else,' she replied irritably. 'I'm it.'

Maggie had no idea how long her morning sickness was going to last but knew she couldn't afford excessive time off work now she was looking down the barrel of single motherhood. Like a million other women before her, she knew she just had to push through.

'Have you had something to eat?' Nash asked, not liking how peaky she was looking.

Maggie placed a hand across her mouth, her stomach revolting at the thought. It gave a funny lurch that, for once, had nothing to do with him. 'Not a good idea right now.'

'It might help.'

She shook her head. At the moment nothing seemed to help. Sleep was the only relief she got. 'Let's just get this over with.' Then she could lose herself in the blissfully nausea-free world of slumber.

'You okay to keep doing this while I change?' she asked.

Nash lifted a navy pack. 'Sure. Almost done.'

They were loaded into a taxi ten minutes later. Maggie tried not to think about what had happened the last time they'd been in a taxi together but it was kind of like not mentioning the elephant in the room. It was there and at least it gave her something else to concentrate on other than her stomach. She wondered if he was thinking about it too.

Thankfully at this early hour traffic was non-existent and they were at the airport in fifteen minutes. Another fifteen minutes saw them airborne.

The noise in the little fixed-wing plane made conversation impossible for which Maggie was glad. Being buckled in next to Nash in the cramped confines was bad enough. She shut her eyes, trying to doze off for the paltry hour and a bit it would take to get to their destination. Trying to cut off the nausea.

Nash inspected her face, her black lashes throwing shadows on her cheekbones. She looked exhausted, her creamy complexion wan, her cheekbones a little more prominent. The pregnancy was obviously already taking its toll on her.

'Here,' he said, raising his voice to be heard over the noise of the engines as he nudged her arm.

Maggie opened her eyes reluctantly, to find Nash holding up a stick of chewing gum. Before she even knew what she was doing she was reaching for it. Something sweet that wouldn't sit in her belly like a rock.

A lifesaver!

'Thanks,' she said, ripping off the wrapper and stuffing it in her mouth before closing her eyes again.

Nash blinked as it disappeared in a few seconds flat. He made a mental note to always have a packet on him. And then he sobered when he remembered that he was only here for a few more weeks.

He'd been thinking a lot the last few days and

wasn't any closer to a solution. But maybe if they actually talked about it. Rationally. They did have an hour.

He lowered his mouth to the vicinity of her ear. 'Are we going to talk or just ignore each other?' he asked.

Maggie opened her eyes and turned to face him. He was disturbingly close, his mouth within easy reach. The gum was having a marvellous effect on her constitution but with all the extraneous noise she really wasn't up to a discussion they'd have to yell at each other anyway.

'Ignore each other,' she confirmed, returning her head to its neutral position and closing her eyes.

Nash smiled despite himself. Okay. She was right. It was hardly the time or place. But they were going to talk about this. Today.

They landed in Rockhampton and took the two-minute taxi ride to the hospital. The pick-up was easy enough. Everything had been done for them. Thanks to the quick actions of a local anaesthetist who'd diagnosed the surgical emergency and performed a tracheostomy, the child just needed transport to a primary care facility where it could be managed further. They were at the Rocky General for half an hour in total.

It was seven a.m. when they pushed through the swing doors of the PICU. Another hour before the patient was settled, notes were written, equipment packed away and they were ready to leave.

'Come on,' Nash said, catching her as she was about to get into her car. 'I'll buy you breakfast.'

Maggie sighed. 'Nash, no. I'm really tired.' She didn't want to rehash what they'd already been through.

He could see that but he wanted this sorted. Now. 'Yes,' he insisted.

'I can't eat anything these days.'

Nash shrugged. 'So I'll eat and you can watch.' He fished in the pocket of his Levi's. 'I have more gum.'

Maggie was about to say no, get in her car and

drive off but then he looked at her with those eyes and said, 'Please, Maggie,' and she folded like a deck of cards.

'Fine,' she huffed.

She followed him to a nearby café precinct and sipped on water while he tucked into a full English breakfast. Maggie watched him eating with gusto. *Plenty of those where he was going.*

The thought of him leaving, of him being on the other side of the world eating authentic English breakfasts while she was here, with his child, loving him, was depressing as hell.

Nash placed his knife and fork on his empty plate and wiped his mouth on a napkin. His full stomach gave him fortitude to face the conversation they needed to have.

'So, Maggie. Where do we go from here?' he asked. 'Have you given any more thought to coming to London with me?'

Had she? She'd thought of little else. And had she been ten years younger and a baby wasn't involved she'd have jumped at it. Thrown caution to the wind and taken the biggest gamble of her life, hoping he would come to love her while accepting that he never might. But this wasn't just about her any more. She had the baby to think about.

'I'm not going to live in London, Nash. I'm sorry, that's just not an option.' She wasn't doing that for anything less than love.

Nash nodded slowly. It had been a long shot— she'd been so adamant the other day. He sighed heavily. 'I understand.'

'We're just going to have to compromise. I know you feel it's your duty to support the baby, right?' Maggie held her breath, waiting for him to deny it. To hear him refute that it was a duty. To hear him say it was an act of love.

'I'm the father,' he said testily. 'Of course it's my duty to support the baby. And you, Maggie.'

Maggie felt another crack splinter the surface of her heart. 'Well, then, we'll work it out. Maybe for those first couple of years, while you're overseas, you can contribute financially. As far as the baby's concerned, they're probably the best years to be away. It won't be aware of you as a father figure until it's much older.'

Nash rubbed his chin, the rough stubble pricking his palm. 'I could try and be here for the birth.'

Maggie swallowed. Now, that would be hard. How was she supposed to keep emotional distance from him during something as intimate as giving birth to his child?

'I could probably come back every few months.'

Maggie could see he was thinking hard about the possibilities and was relieved. She picked up her train of thought. 'Of course,' she agreed. 'And these days there's so many ways that we can keep in touch.'

'You could visit me. Maybe. It wouldn't be much of a picnic, dragging a baby halfway round the world, but I'd pay for you to come first class. I know you're not keen to come to London…'

Maggie was touched by his thoughtfulness and that he was really trying to meet her halfway. Vintage Nash. She was fully aware he could have turned nasty. But she guessed that was the difference between duty and love. It was easy to be removed when deep feelings weren't involved.

'I could probably do a holiday,' she replied. 'Depends on the baby, I guess. If he's—'

'He?' Nash interrupted.

Maggie blushed and placed her hand across her belly. 'Oh, sorry. I just…have a feeling.'

A son. Maggie could be carrying his son. Nash's gaze flicked to her hand splayed against her tummy. 'Will you find out?'

She nodded. 'Yeah, I think I might.'

He wouldn't be here for that. Or to see her belly grow round. And he may well miss the birth. What other things would he miss out on? First words. First steps.

'I can send you the pictures from the ultrasound if you like. And I'll send photos and video footage. You'll probably see more of him than a lot of men do of their kids who live under the same roof.'

Nash considered it. Maybe she was right. It was only for the first couple of years. When he

returned they could work out a better arrange-
ment. Maybe she'd come back home with him.
She might be willing to do that when he was
back in the same country. There'd be nothing to
stop her. Unless… A sudden thought sent a chill
straight up his spine and needling into the base
of his skull.

'What if you meet someone else, Maggie?'
How would he handle another man being a father
to his child? Another man sharing her bed?

Maggie's hand tightened against her stomach
and she forced out a laugh. 'That won't happen.'

He frowned. 'How can you be so sure?'

Because I love you, idiot! Because he'd ruined
her for all men. 'There's no room left in here.'
She tapped her chest. 'It's full up with love for
this little guy. Nothing's more important than
this.' She patted her stomach. 'No one's ever
going to take my focus off him. No one.'

Maggie wished she could wring the same com-
mitment from Nash. The thought of all those
English girls falling for his country-boy charm

had her hovering between deeply depressed and violently jealous. But that had been one of the perils of getting involved with a much younger man. And she'd known it. Nash was young and unattached—he was supposed to be out there, playing the field.

Nash blinked at the conviction in her voice. He believed her. Still, it sounded like a lonely life for her. And for a second he worried that Maggie was shutting herself off from life's possibilities. But then, perversely, as a naked flame of jealousy scorched his veins, he didn't care. He didn't want to ever have to think about another man touching her like he had. To share what they'd shared.

It was selfish. But he didn't care.

The waitress brought the bill and Nash paid it.

'So? What do you think?' Maggie asked as she stood. 'Do you think we've come to a reasonable compromise?'

Nash helped her out with her chair as he mulled over her question. The truth was it didn't sit well with him. It still felt like he was shirking his responsibilities. He doubted his parents would be impressed. But, as she'd said, it was a compromise. He could hardly drag her to London when she didn't want to go.

He had no doubt there was legal recourse but he knew if he forced her to do something she didn't want to do, it could do irreparable damage to their relationship. And she was the mother of his child. It was in both their interests and particularly in the interest of his unborn son—*oh, God he was doing it now*—to keep things amicable.

Hell. How had their fun, easy relationship become so complicated?

'It sounds like a start,' he said.

They walked in silence the short distance to their cars. Maggie turned as she reached for her door handle. 'Should we shake on it?' She held out her hand.

Nash looked at it, then up into her face. She was looking at him with her big brown eyes and he wanted nothing more than to go back to her place and hold her while they fell asleep.

He lifted a hand, stroking her fringe back and tracing her cheekbone until he was cupping her jaw. 'I think we've passed that, don't you?'

His voice was soft and his gaze was on her mouth and she couldn't have stopped her eyes fluttering shut or the sway of her body towards his had her life depended on it. It had been days since he'd kissed her and she yearned for it.

Nash lowered his head and dropped a soft kiss against her pliant lips. Her sigh encouraged him to linger a little longer and he deepened the kiss. But when she moaned he knew they were treading on dangerous ground. She was tired and he knew this wasn't the kind of intimacy she'd allow if she had her wits about her. Not any more.

'Go home, get some sleep,' he whispered against her lips, dragging his mouth away and planting a soft kiss on her forehead before turning away and heading to his car.

Maggie watched him open his door, get in,

start it up and drive away, all the time her heart breaking. How was she ever going to watch him walk away for good?

'What are you wearing to the ball?' Linda asked a few days later as she came round at the start of the late shift to check on how each of her staff members were getting on with their patients. Maggie had been allocated Toby again. She'd developed a real rapport with his parents and a definite soft spot for the little battler.

'Oh, cripes!' Maggie slapped herself on the forehead. 'I've forgotten all about it.' To be fair to herself, she did have quite a bit on her mind and the tickets had been purchased in August.

'I bought myself this swanky little number with a corset-style bodice. Phil's gonna drool all night when he sees it.'

Maggie laughed at her friend. The Christmas Eve ball was not only the highlight of the hospital calendar but the highlight of Linda and Phil's calendar too. Linda's parents took the kids to Carols by Candlelight on the Brisbane River while Linda and Phil lived it up for one night of the year. Of course, they felt like hell at six a.m. when six children landed on their bed demanding to open their presents from Santa.

'I guess I'll need to go shopping for something.'

'Da.' Linda bugged her eyes at Maggie. 'Only seventeen more sleeps.'

Maggie laughed again. 'You're incorrigible.'

'Are you counting down sleeps to Christmas or shopping days remaining?' Nash enquired as he stopped by Maggie's bedside to deliver Toby's latest blood-gas results.

Linda shook her head. 'Neither. Sleeps until the ball,' she informed Nash. 'Although it does help that the kids' Christmas countdown happens to coincide. You are coming, I hope?'

Maggie threw a quick prayer into the ether. Nash in chinos and Levi's was hard enough to ignore. Nash in a tux? Now, that would be a magnificent sight indeed.

'Well I bought my ticket in August but I've got

a morning shift Christmas Day so I'm not sure if it's wise.'

Maggie held her breath. Maybe he wouldn't come?

'Oh, you poor old man,' Linda teased. 'Can't party all night and work the next day any more?'

Nash grinned, responding to Linda's well-intentioned banter but conscious of Maggie growing stiller and stiller beside him. 'Well, I am thirty now.'

'Oh, right. Hey, Maggie's going and she's working the next day. She's got a whole decade on you.'

Maggie winced. She caught Nash's furtive look at her and wished the floor would open and swallow her. She didn't need Linda's reminder of just how idiotic she'd been to think she could play with fire and not get burned.

'I've got to face six children after about two hours' sleep,' Linda continued, oblivious to the currents churning around her. 'And then cook for twenty-six people coming to my house for

Christmas dinner. So don't give me any of your paltry excuses.'

Nash felt horrified, just listening to Linda's Christmas line-up. 'Well, in that case…'

'Good. You can sit at our table,' Linda said patting him on the shoulder. 'Unless you're bringing a partner?'

Maggie swallowed. *Oh, God, he wouldn't, would he?*

Nash caught Maggie's sudden pallor. 'Nope,' he hastened to assure Linda. 'Just me.'

Maggie breathed again. She couldn't have sat at the same table with him while some…female fawned over him.

'It's settled, then.'

'Are you sure?' Nash asked, flicking a brief glance at Maggie, pleased to see some colour had returned to her cheeks, before returning his attention to Linda. 'I don't want to kick anyone off.'

'Of course, we haven't worked out final seating anyway.'

He chanced another glance at Maggie. Her face

was neutral. Hard to read. Did she want him there? Moreover could he sit near her, dressed to the nines without wanting to touch her?

Probably not. 'Thank you. I'd be honoured.'

Maggie was relieved when Nash's pager beeped and he excused himself. Standing next to him, pretending nothing had happened between them, was weird. Standing next to him, knowing she was carrying his child, was plain bizarre.

'Hmm-mmm,' Linda murmured. 'Now there's some eye candy that's gonna look smokin' in a tux.'

Maggie shook her head at her friend's blatant ogling. It felt strange to witness another woman's admiration given how intimately she knew Nash. She even felt a streak of white-hot jealousy stab her in the chest. 'Hey. What about Phil?' she protested.

Linda shook her head. 'I love Phil to death and think he's the most gorgeous man alive. But just cos I'm married, Maggie, it doesn't mean I'm dead. I can appreciate a fine-looking specimen of manhood as much as the next woman. And that man has it in spades.' Linda shook her head. 'They're gonna adore him over there. He's going to break him some English hearts.'

Maggie swallowed. She knew it was the truth. But it hurt. God, how it hurt.

Maggie spent the entire shift trying to get Toby to smile. He looked at her solemnly, his ET tube protruding from his nose like a trunk, his arms wrapped in splints so he couldn't pull it or any of his lines out. He'd been shifted from the high-frequency ventilation back to conventional, which had been a huge step forward. His kidneys were winning the battle and he was having a trial period off the dialysis machine to see if his urine output kept up both in quantity and quality.

Maggie hoped so. Toby had been through a lot in the last weeks and really deserved a lucky break. Nevertheless, she'd gathered all the lines and paraphernalia she'd need for the artificial kidney should he have to go back on overnight.

But, still, he looked miserable. He cried any

time anyone went near him. A mournful silent wail, his blue eyes filling with tears, his little face screwed up in abject misery. Not that Maggie could blame him. He'd been put through the wringer. Tubes and tests and suctioning and X-rays. Taking one step forward only to slide two steps back.

Even his mother was persona non grata with the little boy. Maggie looked up a few hours into the shift and saw her crying. She rounded the bed, put her arm around Alice's shoulders and gave them a quick squeeze.

'He looks at me like I'm the enemy,' she murmured.

'No,' Maggie denied gently as the little boy eyed her like she was going to murder him. 'He reserves that look for the nurses.'

'Well, he looks at me with this look that just says *why?* Why are you letting them do it to me?'

'I know,' Maggie murmured. 'He's young and he can't possibly understand. He's been through a lot, Alice. He's been very sick but he's clawing his way back. His humour will improve as he starts to feel better.'

Alice wiped her eyes. 'I know,' she said reaching out and squeezing Toby's hand. 'Thanks, Maggie. You have no idea how much we appreciate the support you guys give us. You're angels, all of you.'

Maggie had never been comfortable with how people equated nurses with angels. Yes, she loved her job and she liked to think she went above and beyond. But she was human with human failings. At no time was that more evident than right now as the ever-present nausea twisted through her gut.

Alice popped out a couple of hours later and Maggie sat with Toby as he cried great silent sobs and looked behind him, searching for his mother. She read to him for a bit and then tried to interest him a game of peek-a-boo.

'Oh, dear, Toby's not a happy camper.'

Maggie looked up as Nash approached the other side of Toby's bed. 'No. He's not.

Nash reached for a glove. 'I think Toby needs a pet fish,' he said. He scrunched the opening together like the neck of a balloon and blew into it. The glove, including the five fingers, inflated, looking like an udder.

Toby stopped crying and watched the process warily. Nash tied the end where he'd blown into and then inverted it. He took his pen out of his pocket and drew in some scales and two eyes. It now looked like some bizarre mutant fish with a pointy nose and giant spines. But at least it looked like a fish.

'Ta-da,' Nash announced. He watched the mistrust on Toby's face. 'Tough crowd,' he remarked to Maggie.

Maggie smiled. She was touched that Nash, in that special way of his, was trying and had at least halted Toby's heart-wrenching sobs. 'I think your fish is lonely,' she said, looking away from Nash towards Toby. 'I think he needs a friend.' And she reached for a glove.

'Aha.' Nash nodded. 'A girlfriend.'

Maggie stopped in mid-blow and looked at Nash, but he wasn't looking at her so she hastily constructed her own fish.

'Here, I'll do the scales,' Nash volunteered.

Maggie handed it over and waited while he drew kissy, fishy lips, eyes with long curly eyelashes and scales that looked like they belonged on a mermaid. He winked at her as he handed it back. 'What do you think, Toby?'

Toby's gaze shifted from one to the other as Nash and Maggie swam the fish through the air, making nonsense noises and silly fishy conversation in funny voices. Toby finally reached for a fish.

'Progress.' Nash smiled as he handed his creation over. Toby took it and almost, *almost* smiled.

'Ha! Did you see that?' Maggie grinned at Nash. 'He nearly smiled. I'm not giving up on you, young man.' Maggie wagged her finger playfully at Toby, who frowned at her.

Nash grinned back. 'We make a good team.'

Maggie's smile faded a little. Where would he be when their child was fractious? What if he fell ill?

No, no, no. She wouldn't go there. She could do this on her own. She could. She would not get maudlin on the back of such a sweet, if small, victory.

They watched Toby staring at the fish for a moment or two. He even wiggled it a little and they both gave him encouraging nods. Nash looked over at Maggie, sitting on the opposite side of the bed. She looked happy. Really happy that they'd been able to allay Toby's misery for a while. If ever there was a woman fit to be a mother, it was her.

He looked around him for a moment and then turned back to her. 'You don't mind about the ball, do you? About Linda asking me to join your table?'

Maggie looked up from Toby. Being near him that night was going to be hell. 'Of course not,' she murmured, looking back at Toby. 'I'm really good with our decision,' she lied. 'There's no reason why we can't enjoy a social night together. We're adults, Nash. It'll be fine.'

After all, she was going to have to get used to

him being in her life. She'd never be able to chalk their relationship up to a moment of weakness. *Or madness.* Not now. As hard as it was, they were inextricably joined. She may as well start practising her this-doesn't-bother-me countenance. She had a feeling she was going to need to use it.

Often.

CHAPTER EIGHT

'ONE MORE SLEEP.'

Maggie rolled her eyes at Linda as she checked her six-o'clock antibiotics. She was glad that she wouldn't have to hear the countdown again for another twelve months. 'How old are you?'

'Oh, come on, Scrooge,' Linda teased. 'You love it too.'

Yes. She usually did. But this was not going to be a normal hospital ball. She was pregnant. And the father of the baby was going to be at the same table. In a tux.

'They look good to me,' Maggie said, deliberately changing the subject. She clicked on the medication chart and it opened on the monitor screen, allowing her to sign that she'd checked the drugs. 'How's Christopher going?' she asked as she typed in her password. She was in charge of the afternoon shift and needed to keep up to date with the patients' conditions.

'We're just waiting on his formal bloods. His kidney function is holding but his haemoglobin is falling. His last pulmonary haemorrhages didn't help. We're going to transfuse if it's less than seventy.'

Maggie nodded and moved to the other side of the bed where Christopher's mother sat, holding her heavily sedated son's hand. The teenager was very pale. 'How are you doing, Bree?' she asked, placing a hand on the woman's shoulder.

'Okay, I guess,' she said, looking up at Maggie. 'I still can't believe it, though. I know we've been here for quite a few days now but I just can't wrap my head around it.'

Maggie nodded. Five days ago fourteen-year-old Christopher Thirkettle had coughed up large amounts of blood at school and collapsed. He'd been brought to the Brisbane Children's Hospital via ambulance where his condition had deteriorated down in the accident department requiring him to be intubated and ventilated.

A battery of tests had revealed that the teenager had Goodpasture's disease, a very rare autoimmune disorder that caused the body's immune system to attack its own lung and kidney tissue. After months of vague flu-like symptoms, lethargy and a dry cough his deterioration had been rapid.

The kidney component of the disease hadn't progressed at this stage and they were monitoring it very carefully, hoping to arrest its development altogether. Unfortunately, though, despite commencing steroids, his lungs were still in a bad way and he'd had several pulmonary haemorrhages in the last few days.

'It's perfectly normal to have feelings of disbelief when your child falls ill like this,' Maggie assured Bree, giving her shoulder a squeeze. 'Would you like to chat to our social worker to talk some of these feelings through? I can arrange it for you.'

'That won't be necessary, Sister.'

Maggie turned to find Christopher's rather overbearing grandfather behind her. He was an odd man, often rude and abrupt, but he'd lived with Christopher and Bree since his grandson had been a baby and there was no denying how good he was with Christopher. She took a deep, steadying breath.

'Dad,' Bree said softly. 'Maggie's just trying to help.'

'Well anyway,' Maggie said, 'just let me know if you ever require their services.' She gave Bree's shoulder another squeeze and moved back towards Linda, keeping one ear on the conversation between father and daughter.

'Are the results back yet?' he asked.

'Not yet, Dad.'

'I think it's a mistake to give him a blood transfusion. We don't know what diseases could be passed on to him.'

'Dad, we've been through this,' Bree muttered. 'Leave it alone.'

Maggie shared a look with Linda. Bree had let them know in the beginning that her father was a control freak and a conspiracy theorist. He'd been under the care of a psychiatrist for long periods of depression since his wife, Bree's mother, had passed away years ago from a hospital bungle.

She'd warned them that her father would find Christopher's hospitalisation difficult.

And she hadn't been wrong. He had been quite trying, questioning the necessity for every single treatment, every blood test, every X-ray and drug.

Being allocated to Christopher's bed was fast becoming something to avoid. Bree was great but her father was trying everyone's patience.

Still, it was all part of the job and Maggie knew that underneath the man's incessant badgering and tendency to interfere he was basically a concerned grandfather and a grieving husband who hadn't worked through his issues from his wife's death. Everyone reacted differently when their loved ones were critically ill and the PICU staff

were well used to dealing with the many mani-
festations of grief.

'You okay here?' she asked Linda quietly.

Linda nodded. 'I'll be fine. I'll holler if I need
you.'

Maggie moved to bed three to check out
Toby's progress. The nurse looking after him
took advantage of Maggie's presence and
scooted to the bathroom.

Maggie greeted Brett and then turned her attention to Toby. 'Hello, little man,' she crooned,
moving to the opposite side of the bed from his
father. 'Have you got a smile for me yet?'

'Nope. Still cranky with the world, I'm afraid.'
Brett grimaced.

'Ah, well.' Maggie smiled at the little boy
whose bottom lip was wobbling. 'I guess he has
a right to be.'

But he was improving rapidly each day. He
hadn't needed to go back on dialysis and despite
being stuck for weeks with his ventilation, even
that was now improving with some good

progress being made with weaning. The monotonous, worrying holding pattern had lifted as Toby's condition turned a corner. Everyone was hoping that Alice and Brett's Christmas present would be a newly extubated son.

She picked up Toby's foot and waggled her fingers against his toes. Toby's face scrunched up as he started to cry, tugging his leg out of her grasp.

Brett laughed. 'Sorry.'

Maggie gave him a rueful smile. 'It's okay. Us PICU nurses know we're not exactly popular with our patients.'

'No, but the parents think you're marvellous.'

Maggie smiled at him. It was great to see Toby's parents looking so positive. Toby's nurse returned and Maggie excused herself. She went to check on the staff in the side rooms but was temporarily waylaid by the colourful sight of the Christmas tree. With only two more days till Christmas the bottom of the tree was crowded with gaily wrapped Secret Santa presents.

'Looks fantastic, doesn't it?' Nash murmured near her ear.

Maggie felt a trail of goose-bumps march down her arm. 'Magnificent.'

Nash knelt and started sifting through the presents. 'Now, where is it?' he mused.

'Hey,' Maggie objected. 'What are you doing?'

'Finding my present and trying to work out what it is,' he said matter-of-factly.

Maggie pulled at his collar. 'You're not supposed to do that.'

'Sure you are. That's half the fun.'

Maggie shook her head at him. He looked like a little kid. He was incorrigible. Just as well he wasn't going to be around for their baby. She could just imagine him teaching their son a whole bunch of endearingly naughty things. Being fun Daddy and leaving her to be the bad guy.

'Aha! Here it is.' Nash stood brandishing his present. 'It's a bit small,' he murmured, giving the hard rectangular box-shaped gift a shake.

Maggie shrugged. 'Good things come in small packages.'

Nash looked down at her. 'I know.' He heard a satisfying little rattle as he continued to shake it. 'Hmm, I wonder what it is?'

Maggie knew. She couldn't believe it when she had drawn Nash in the Secret Santa draw. Buying a gift for someone for five dollars was hard enough, but for Nash? The man she loved.

She'd searched high and low, trying to find just the right thing, hoping that he'd be able to see the depth of her feelings in the perfect gift. When she'd stumbled into an Australiana store in the city and found eucalyptus-impregnated gum nuts for sale she knew she'd found exactly what she'd been looking for. Something to remind him of home. The bush. And maybe of her.

Nash grinned at her. 'Let's find yours.'

'No,' Maggie protested as Nash knelt again. 'I'll leave it for the twenty-fifth, thanks very much,' she said primly, and departed, removing herself from temptation. Of Nash, not the tree.

Twenty minutes later Nash tracked her down in the tearoom. 'Christopher's results are back. His haemoglobin is sixty-four. I've organised the cross-match with the lab. They're going to ring us when the blood's ready.'

Maggie nodded. 'Have you told Bree?'

Nash easily read between the lines. He knew what she was really asking was, *Does the grandfather know?* 'I've told Bree. And her father.'

'How'd that go?'

'He's not happy.'

Maggie felt a slight edge of worry and hoped he wasn't going to be a problem. 'Well, thankfully it isn't up to him.'

Nash nodded. 'I did explain again that it was vital. That Christopher's low haemoglobin level has a direct effect on the oxygen-carrying capacity of the blood and with his lungs being so sick it was interfering with his body's oxygenation.'

'What'd he say to that?'

'He thinks we could give him more iron tablets. And spinach.'

Maggie almost choked on her cup of tea. 'What?'

'I know.' Nash nodded. Christopher's anaemia was way beyond being benefited by any pharmaceutical or nutritional intervention. Especially with the potential for further pulmonary haemorrhages. 'Anyway, as you say, Bree's given her consent and that's all that matters.'

'Okay.' Maggie nodded. 'Thanks for trying.'

An hour later Maggie took a call from the blood bank to tell her they'd put two units of cross-matched blood in the blood fridge for Christopher. Maggie glanced over at bed five. Bree was there but her ever-present father was outside, having a break. Now was a good time to get the blood up— less hassle without Christopher's grandfather and his disapproving presence.

Linda was on her break and due back in ten minutes. Nash had gone to Radiology with Gemma Perkins, the PICU director, to discuss a case. He shouldn't be too much longer either. If she went and got the blood now, she and Linda could check it and put it up together with as little fuss as possible, and Nash would be here to deal with any grandfather-related issues.

'Ray, I'm just going to the blood fridge.'

Maggie had allocated Ray and Gwen as runners. It was their job to be the gophers for the staff looking after the patients as it was policy in PICU that no patient was ever left unattended.

'Sure thing,' Ray said.

As Maggie pushed though the swing doors of the unit she heard singing and was delighted to see that the choir that visited the hospital every night in the lead-up to Christmas had stopped outside the PICU parents' lounge.

The entire floor was often overlooked as out-siders were hesitant about approaching the unit. But Maggie knew one thing for sure—PICU parents were probably the most stressed parents in the hospital. If anyone needed a little light en-tertainment, it was them.

They sang 'Ding Dong Merrily on High' and Maggie lingered for a moment, listening to the superb voices and feeling a sense of peace on earth and goodwill to all men. She looked around at the parents who had come outside to listen and was gratified to see smiles.

'They're good, aren't they?'

Maggie looked beside her to see Christopher's grandfather watching as he peeled an orange. 'Yes.'

'Where are you off to?' he asked.

Maggie darted him a quick look. While she didn't want the hassle of him being alerted to the imminent transfusion, she wasn't going to lie or sneak around. Christopher needed the blood. It was a medically indicated intervention and she would not let one cranky old man compromise her patient's condition.

'To the blood fridge,' she said, keeping her voice calm and neutral. But she saw his lips thin and his fingers tighten around the orange and for the first time instead of feeling annoyed she felt a little creepy.

'Bree's wrong to allow this,' he muttered. 'I've read the reports the government tries to cover up.

He could end up with HIV or Hep B. You could be passing on a death sentence.'

'Mr Thirkettle, as Dr Reece has already explained, blood transfusions are screened for both HIV and Hep B.'

'What about that mad cow's disease? There's no test for it.'

'No, but the donors are screened,' Maggie said patiently. They'd been through this several times over the last few days. 'It's a very safe, very effective treatment. Your grandson needs this transfusion.'

He shook his head. 'Bree should never have given her consent.'

'Your daughter is following medical advice.'

'Hmph! Doctors,' he sneered. 'They've got it wrong in the past. Just ask my poor Lizzy.'

Maggie was a little chilled by the utter disdain and tinge of hatred she heard in his voice. Her feelings of goodwill vanished as she began to really worry that he might attempt to stop the transfusion going ahead. She made a mental note to ring Security and alert them to the potential threat when she got back to the unit.

Great, just what she needed! Just what Bree needed—her father being carted off by security.

She excused herself as the choir took its leave, putting the altercation behind her. It took all sorts, Maggie lectured herself as she turned in the opposite direction from the singers and walked along the practically deserted corridors of the hospital to the blood fridge. It was nearly eight o'clock and thanks to Christopher's grandfather she was now counting down the minutes until the end of her shift. Ninety, to be exact.

She used her swipe card to access the room where the fresh blood products were kept. The loud hum from the fridge's motor greeted her and echoed around the confined space. Maggie opened the heavy door and searched through the various trays until she found Christopher's bags. The top one had the lab form attached and she pulled it out, signed for it in the book beside the fridge and then let herself out of the room.

She was almost back when she rounded a corner to find Christopher's grandfather sitting in one of the low chairs that had been strategically placed on every floor near the lifts to create a lounge-type area. He rose to his feet quickly when he saw her and she stopped abruptly.

'Is that it?' he asked, nodding towards the bag of blood she had in her hand.

Maggie's heart thumped loudly as she felt a prickle of danger lift the hairs on her neck. She edged closer, her gaze darting over his shoulder. 'Yes.' She swallowed.

'I'm going to appeal to your compassionate side now, Nurse, and ask you not to do this.'

She edged again slowly trying to get to the other side of him. He hadn't given her any reason to suspect that he'd hurt anyone but this was definitely threatening behaviour. 'Okay,' she reasoned. 'Let's go back to the unit and we can discuss it with Dr Reece again.'

He shook his head. 'I can't let you do that.' Maggie moved again and he motioned her to stop. 'I can't let them harm Christopher like they did Lizzy.'

Maggie tried to figure out how far she had to go to angle herself in a position where she could run. 'We're trying to help him, Mr Thirkettle,' she said. Maybe if she kept him talking she could inch her way around him. Or someone else might come along. She'd give anything to see Nash now.

'He doesn't need that kind of help.'

Maggie was so focused on her goal that she didn't really heed the sinister drop in his voice. Her gaze flicked past him again. 'Okay. We can sit down again and talk it through back on the unit.'

'Do you have kids, Nurse?'

Maggie was halfway to her goal, her leg brushing the lounge chair. His comment reminded her that it wasn't just herself that was in peril here. She had a life growing inside her, her own child, and she'd was damned if this man was going to jeopardise that in any way. 'Look, this is really inappropriate Mr—'

'I don't care about that,' he roared.

Maggie jumped as his voice cracked across the short space that separated them. He looked crazy suddenly and she knew she was in trouble.

His voice dropped again. 'I'm sorry but I just can't let you do this.'

Maggie's heart was practically jumping out of her chest and her eyes bugged as he pulled a knife, the one he'd been peeling the orange with, out of his pocket.

'Wait,' Maggie pleaded, holding out her hand to ward him off as he advanced towards her. 'Here, take it,' she said holding it out to him. One bag of blood wasn't worth her life.

'Oh, I'll take it all right,' he snarled, and raised his knife-wielding hand.

Maggie held her crossed arms up to protect herself, protect the baby as he slashed towards her with the knife. She was terrified, utterly terrified. The knife came into contact with the bag and freezing cold blood gushed from the ruptured plastic and ran all down her and pooled on the linoleum floor.

Maggie could smell the metallic scent mingle with that of her own fear as the moment seemed frozen in time. He wrenched the bag out of her hands, knocking her backwards in the process. Maggie tried to regain her balance but slipped in the sticky mess at her feet.

She twisted, cried out, fell and hit her head on the hard wooden arm of the lounge chair on the way down. Maggie heard the vague clattering of the knife and saw it land not far from her head in her peripheral vision before everything went black and she lost consciousness.

Nash and Gemma had finished in Radiology and were discussing Nash's move to Great Ormond Street Hospital when Linda caught up with them, a bag of chips and a can of soft drink in hand.

'Been raiding the machine?' Gemma asked.

Linda nodded. 'I was over visiting a friend on ward two. And you know me, Gemma, can't go by that damn machine without sampling the wares.'

'Well, all proceeds do go to Radio Giggle,'

Gemma pointed out. 'So really you're just making a charitable donation.'

Linda laughed. 'Hey, yeah, you're right.'

They reached the end of their corridor and turned right. Nash noticed some smudges on the floor. 'What's that?' He frowned.

They all looked down. 'Looks like a bloody footprint,' Linda mused.

Nash looked up, noticing they disappeared around the corner they were soon to take. He looked behind him in the opposite direction, tracking them with his eyes as they travelled the length of the corridor.

'Someone might have cut their foot,' Linda suggested.

Nash nodded but had a strange itch up his spine as they followed the trail. The wall had a bloody handprint just before they rounded the corner.

'Curious and curiouser,' Gemma murmured.

Nash was the first to see Maggie, followed closely by Linda's gasp. His heart almost stopped in his chest as his shocked brain, already reeling from seeing a body on the floor surrounded in blood, realised it was Maggie.

'Maggie?' He ran to her side, kneeling in the blood, uncaring of his clothes or getting blood on himself. His mind raced, trying to sort through all possible scenarios. What the hell had happened? Where had all this blood come from? Nash didn't think he'd ever seen so much in his life.

'Maggie.' He shook her this time.

Gemma felt for a carotid. 'Good pulse.'

Nash felt some of the edge to his panic dissipate but then Linda said, 'Oh, no.' She held up a bloodied knife and Nash felt sick. Someone had stabbed her?

'I'll call the crash team and Security,' Gemma said pulling her mobile out of her pocket.

Nash yanked out the heavy-duty scissors he carried in a pouch on his belt and in a couple of seconds had sheared through Maggie's polo shirt. Her white bra was soaked red as he ran his hands all over her abdomen and chest searching for a wound. The feel of her warm congealing blood made him more and more frantic.

When he couldn't find an entry point, he sheared through each leg of her trousers and repeated the exercise, looking for the bleeding point.

'This amount of blood has to indicate a major vessel, Nash,' Gemma said as she too tried to locate where the fresh-looking blood was coming from.

Nash's movements grew more frantic. He felt like he was watching the life force ebb from her, could smell her blood all around him, and he wanted to pick her up and hug her to him. Shake her. Tell her not to leave him.

'Nowhere. There's nowhere,' Gemma said. 'Where else could she be bleeding from?'

Then Nash knew. The baby. *Oh, God, was she miscarrying?* Had she haemorrhaged and fainted? A fresh wave of panic hit him. 'She's pregnant,' he said, looking up at Gemma.

Gemma and Linda stared at him like he'd lost his mind. 'Are you sure?' Linda asked.

Nash nodded. 'It's mine. I'm sure.'

There were a couple more seconds when they continued to look at him in disbelief but then Maggie started to stir and everything was forgotten.

'Maggie?' Nash felt his heart leap in his chest as she moved her head and groaned.

'Maggie, it's Gemma. Can you open your eyes?'

Maggie's head was thumping and Gemma's voice sounded very far away but she prised her eyes open obediently. Gemma swam in and out of focus.

'Maggie!'

Nash? 'Nash? What's wrong?' She tried to sit up but hands held her down. 'What happened?' she asked dazedly.

'Were you stabbed? Where, Maggie? Where were you stabbed?' Nash ran his hands over her again looking for a wound.

Maggie frowned as her head continued to throb. 'What? No.' The events came flooding back. She struggled to sit and was held down again. She became aware of the congealing blood sticking to her arms, caking on her body. 'He didn't stab me,' she protested. 'He got the bag of blood. Not me.'

'He who?' Linda demanded.

'Christopher's grandfather. He slashed the bag and then ripped it off me and ran. I fell…slipped in the blood and hit my head, that's all.' Maggie lifted her hand to her head to try and ease the jackhammers drilling into her skull.

The crash team, consisting of an A and E doctor and two of their nurses, an anaesthetist and two wardsmen along with three burly security guards, burst through the nearby fire escape door. Ray arrived as part of the PICU response at the same time. They all froze as they took in the scene.

Had Maggie's head not throbbed so much she might have laughed. She guessed it did rather look like a massacre had just occurred. And then they all moved at once and there was pandemonium in the corridor.

The head security officer called for back-up and made a call to the police. He sent his two officers to search for the perpetrator. Gemma organised the wardies to get a gurney and sent the A and E staff back to their department. Linda organised Ray to take charge of the unit and two of the newly arrived security officers went with him.

Maggie looked at Nash who was looking even worse than the morning he'd found the positive pregnancy test in her bathroom. He was running his bloodied hands through his hair and a smear of blood marred one otherwise perfect cheek. 'Nash?'

Nash heard her small voice, usually so firm and assured, and he hauled her into a sitting position and tucked her into his chest. She was trembling and he hugged her closer. He didn't care that he'd have even more blood over him or that the hand he had on her head, stroking her hair, was covered in the red sticky stuff. She was okay. The baby was okay. That was all that mattered.

'Bloody hell, Maggie, you scared the living daylights out of me.'

Maggie rested her cheek against his shirt. It felt heavenly against her thumping temple and she turned her face into his shirt, smelling the essence of him, eliminating the sickly metallic aroma playing havoc with her nausea.

'Come on, you two,' Linda interrupted. 'We need to get Maggie to X-Ray.'

Maggie looked at Nash and shook her head. 'No, Nash, I can't,' she whispered. 'The baby,' she mouthed.

Nash smiled and dropped a kiss on her nose, elated to see her sitting and talking and thinking and being all Maggie and bossy. For an awful moment he'd thought she was dead. 'I'm afraid they know about the baby, Maggie.'

Maggie gaped at him. She would have been really mad had it not hurt her head, and Gemma and Linda were grinning stupidly at her so she just rolled her eyes. 'Well, okay, then. So I'm not having an X-ray.'

Gemma cocked an eyebrow at Nash. 'Maggie, you were knocked out. For quite a while. We need to check you didn't do some damage.'

Maggie squirmed out of his embrace and tried

to get to her feet on legs that felt like jelly. Nash helped her. As soon as she was up she pulled her elbow out of his grasp. 'I'm fine,' she said. Unfortunately a wave of dizziness chose that moment to assail her and she swayed.

'Whoa.' Nash caught her, sweeping her up off her feet with Maggie protesting the entire way. The gurney arrived at the same time and he placed her on it. 'See?' he said gently.

'No X-ray,' she said mutinously. 'Do a full neuro assessment if you must, but I'm not irradiating this baby.'

'Maggie,' Gemma appealed. 'One X-ray is not going to hurt the baby. They'll take appropriate precautions.'

'No.'

'You'll have to stay overnight for observation if you refuse,' Gemma lectured.

Maggie looked at the two doctors, united in their determination to expose her baby to deadly radiation. 'Fine.'

* * *

Two hours later Nash was finally free to leave work and visit Maggie. She'd been whisked away by ambulance to the Brisbane General while he'd been held up with the police and handing over to Mac. Every instinct he'd owned had rebelled against their separation but he'd known hospital was the best place for her.

Still, the sight of her lying in that pool of blood kept running through his head with sickening clarity and the need to reassure himself that she was okay was paramount. He was increasingly frustrated by the amount of time it was taking and his nerves were stretched to breaking point when he finally managed to get away.

She was tucked up asleep when he entered her private room. She was wearing one of those awful hospital gowns and looked pale and fragile against the white sheets. An ugly mark marred her left temple, a purple bruise embellishing it further. At least the blood was gone. Nash didn't think he'd ever be able to scrub that image from his mind.

He dropped a light kiss on her forehead but she didn't stir. He pulled up a chair close to the bed, sank into it and reached for her nearest hand. She still didn't stir. Nash could feel the warmth of her palm in his and see her chest rising and falling so he knew she was okay, but her stillness was almost as sickening as the blood.

Nash rested his chin on the bed and watched. He watched her deep, even respirations. The bound of her abdominal pulse. The fluttering of her eyes beneath her lids. He watched, relieved, overwhelmingly thankful that she was okay.

A nurse came in and smiled at Nash. She did a set of neuro obs and Nash leaned closer as Maggie stirred to the nurse's insistent demand that she open her eyes.

'Nash?' Maggie murmured, becoming aware of his presence just as retinal-detaching light was blasted into her pupils. Nash was here? The thought helped soothe the ache a little and she threaded her fingers through his.

'I'm here,' he said, squeezing her hand.

Maggie answered a series of questions the nurse fired at her and dutifully moved all her limbs. 'How's your head?'

'Feels like someone's drilling a hole in it with a jackhammer.' Maggie grimaced.

'I can get you something for it,' the nurse suggested.

Maggie shifted her free hand to her belly and splayed her fingers there. 'No, thanks. I'll cope.'

'A couple of Panadol aren't going to hurt, Maggie,' Nash interceded.

'I'm fine.'

'Okay, then. See you in an hour,' the nurse said as she left.

Maggie's head throbbed. 'Oh, goody,' she muttered as her eyes fluttered shut.

Nash chuckled. It was good to see Maggie's humour was intact. 'You could have had the X-ray,' he chided.

Maggie could feel herself drifting off to sleep again and let it slide. A nagging question pulled her out and her eyes struggled open. She rolled her head to the side to find Nash's gaze firmly trained on her. 'Did they get him?'

Nash nodded. 'Yes, he's been apprehended.'

Maggie pursed her lips, the whole crazy jumble of events too much for her sore head to contemplate. Her lids drifted downwards again. *No, wait, there was something else.* She forced her eyes open. 'Did Christopher get his transfusion?'

Nash shook his head. Trust Maggie to be thinking of one of her patients in the midst of all of this. 'Yes. He did. Bree popped in to visit you but you were asleep.'

Maggie smiled as she felt the tug of sleep pulling her under. 'Not her fault,' she murmured.

Nash watched her drift away, her grip on his hand easing, grateful that despite her ordeal she was still the same Maggie. His mobile buzzed in his pocket and he slowly extricated himself so he could switch it off.

Maggie, teetering on the edge of the precipice between light sleep and total oblivion, felt his withdrawal as if her safety rope had been tugged away and her eyes flew open as her heart rate spiked. 'No,' she murmured, reaching for his hand. 'Don't leave.'

She felt an edge of panic swell up. *Not yet. I have another few weeks with you. Don't leave me yet.*

'Hey, shh, it's okay,' Nash said, ignoring his phone as she clawed his hand back into her grasp, holding it prisoner against her belly. 'I'm not going anywhere.'

He smiled at her and Maggie's pulse settled again as the panic receded and the imprint of his hand against her abdomen registered. She shut her eyes. 'Yes, you are.'

The words were her last as this time sleep tugged her completely under.

Nash blinked at the streak of accusation in her mumbled words. *Yes, you are.*

Did she want him to stay?

Her stomach was warm beneath his palm as Nash turned her words over in his head. He recognised the flat contours he'd grown to know so well in such a short time and felt a pang that he wasn't going to get to see her shape change, feel the roundness replace the smooth planes.

It was the first time he'd touched her in any intimate way in weeks, and the fact that his child lay beneath their hands made it even more intimate. His mind returned to the awful events and plagued him with what-ifs, and his hand tightened against her belly.

What if she'd really been stabbed? What if the baby had been injured? What if she'd died? What if something like this had happened while he was living overseas? He shuddered, thinking about it, and the feeling that he was shirking his duties returned with a vengeance as her *Yes, you are* mingled with the emotions of the night's events.

Except it was about more than duty now. This was real. Maggie was real. The baby beneath his hands was real. It didn't feel like a problem that had to be solved suddenly or a responsibility he had to bear. So what *was* it?

Maybe he was becoming a father?

Seeing Maggie like that on the floor—still and

bleeding—had stirred something in him. Shifted something. The thought that the baby might be in danger had been equally as dreadful. Maybe his caveman protective instincts were kicking in? His woman, his child. His job to protect them.

But how could he do that from the other side of the world?

Yes, you are.

Nash groaned and laid his forehead on the crisp white sheet. This made no sense. They'd already figured out what they were going to do. And Maggie had seemed really happy. At peace with it. Except her grip on his hand and her mumbled words just now seemed to refute that.

His career plans and his future dreams inspired by his sister's struggle warred with the emotions that flooded him as he sat here looking at Maggie.

What the hell was happening to him?

CHAPTER NINE

MAGGIE STIRRED EARLY the next morning and stared down at Nash's golden hair. It took a moment to orientate herself. She'd shuffled down the bed overnight and was lying on her side, facing Nash, in a foetal position. Their heads were quite close, one of his hands tucked into hers, cradled in the juncture between her curled belly and tucked-up thighs. His head was angled awkwardly towards her, his right cheek against the sheets, his gorgeous face relaxed in slumber.

The usual wave of morning sickness appeared to be absent so she took a moment to just gaze at him. Her love swelled in her chest and she savoured the moment, knowing there would be no more of these. She felt strangely emotional as the impact of last night hit her anew. Before she could stop herself, she leaned forward and dropped a light kiss against his mouth.

Nash woke up abruptly. He'd slept fitfully all night with the constant interruptions from the nurses and had only fallen into a deeper sleep in the last couple of hours as the neuro obs had gone to four-hourly. Still, he was instantly awake at the brush of her lips.

'Hi.' She smiled as he raised his head off the bed like he'd been hit with a taser. 'Sorry. Couldn't resist it. Bad Maggic.'

Nash's thundering heart rate settled as he realised everything was okay. He smiled back at her and laid his head down again. 'She's my favourite.'

Maggie laughed and the dull throb behind her eyes gave a vicious pulse. She winced.

'Head still hurt?'

'Only when I laugh,' she murmured. 'It's much better. I feel much better.'

Nash let his gaze roam around her face. Her colour was back and apart from the bruise-encased graze on her temple she looked essentially normal. She'd certainly had more sleep than he'd had.

He lifted a hand and brushed her fringe off her forehead. 'You scared me, Maggie May.'

Maggie's heart squeezed painfully in her chest at his endearment. 'I was pretty damn scared myself.'

'Don't do that to me again.'

Maggie looked at him. *How would he know?* But she remembered his face from last night and cut him some slack. Their situation sucked and she had no one but herself to blame. 'Deal.'

The night nurse bustled in for her last set of obs and Maggie sat up. Nash missed her immediately. He'd always loved waking up next to her and this morning hadn't been any different. In fact after last night, it had been an absolute joy.

'When does the doctor do his round?' Maggie asked her.

'He should be around before lunch,' the nurse said.

Maggie frowned. 'That long?'

'You've got somewhere to be?' Nash asked, amused by her Maggie-like annoyance.

'I've got the ball tonight.'

Nash rubbed his hand along the stubble that had peppered his jaw overnight. 'Ah. I don't think so.'

Maggie raised an eyebrow. 'I'm sorry?'

Nash sighed. 'Maggie. You have a concussion. Don't give me any grief over this.'

'I'm fine.'

'You need to be resting.'

'He's right,' the nurse admitted as she recorded Maggie's pupillary reaction in the chart at the end of the bed.

Maggie gave her the eyebrow this time and she wisely backed out of the room. 'I'm fine,' she repeated, turning her attention back to him.

Nash took her hand. 'It'll be too tiring.'

'I slept like a rock last night.'

Nash nodded. 'Yes. It's called concussion.'

Maggie wormed herself out of his grasp. 'I bumped my head, I didn't have a lobotomy.'

'Maggie, you know the doctor's going to advise against it.'

Maggie wasn't sure why she was so desperate to go suddenly when only yesterday she'd been thinking how hard it would be to sit near Nash, *Nash in a tux,* and know he was leaving. But she'd just be sitting at home, doing it. Keeping busy was the only way she was going to get through the months until the baby was born. After that she figured she'd be too busy to think about anything.

And then there was the dress. She'd bought it a few days ago and knew she looked spectacular in it. She'd already pictured a thousand times the look on Nash's face when he first saw her in it. The look that told her she was his, that covered her in his heavy emotional fingerprints, that said, *Hey, baby let's blow this joint and go swap DNA.*

It was the closest thing to love she was ever going to see on his face and, damn it, she wanted to see it again. She wanted to dress up for him. Wanted to show Nash just what he was kissing goodbye.

'I'm going to be in a roomful of doctors and nurses. Hell, the neurologist will probably be there. I couldn't be in a better place.'

'You should be tucked up in bed. Fast asleep.' He added the last bit for his own sake. Maggie tucked up in bed never involved anything as passive as sleeping in his head.

'What are you going to do, Nash? Lock me in my room?'

Nash knew he had no power to stop her but couldn't help the overwhelming feeling that it was his job to protect her. From herself, if need be. He gave a rueful smile. 'Don't be putting thoughts in my head, Maggie May.'

Maggie sucked in a breath. His pupils had dilated and she felt the familiar tug in her womb. 'Please, Nash?' Not that she needed his permission but she wouldn't put it past him to try and influence the medical decision to discharge her.

Nash wavered. 'Maybe for a short time?'

Maggie nodded eagerly.

'And no dancing.'

She nodded again. 'I'll even stick to orange juice.'

'Damn straight you will,' he muttered. 'And I'm staying with you tonight.'

Maggie gave him an oh-will-you-now look. 'Do you think my concussion is up to that?'

'In a purely professional capacity, of course.'

Maggie smiled. *Not if she could help it.* If she could manage the ball, she could certainly manage what would inevitably come next if they were under the same roof. 'Of course.'

Maggie smoothed the bodice of the dress flat against her stomach for the hundredth time as she waited for Nash to arrive. She inspected her image from all angles in her dressing-table mirror. It was the sort of outfit that clung and had she been even another month along, she couldn't have worn it.

She checked her watch, pleased that she'd been able to get herself ready in such a short time. She hadn't been discharged till close to four and managing to convince Nash she'd be okay to get ready without him hovering like a mother hen had taken another hour. She'd finally kicked him out at five-thirty, insisting he go home and get ready himself then come back and pick her up.

A knock sounded on the door and she felt the ball of nerves in her stomach tangle a little tighter. She gave herself a quick once-over and made her way through the house, switching out lights as she went.

Nash could see her coming towards him through the glass panels in the door and almost sagged against it in relief. He'd been nervous about leaving her alone and had torn home, showered quickly, thrown his clothes on and roared back. His heart had pounded as he'd strode up the path and before knocking he'd spent a second calculating how easy it would be to kick the door in if Maggie didn't answer within the minute.

All his macho protective instincts, however, died a quick death when she opened the door. He went from picturing her lying unconscious some-where in the house to picturing himself tearing her dress off and throwing her on the bed.

'Wow.'

She looked amazing. Her satiny off-white floor-length gown looked very Rita Hayworth. Its halter neck dipped to reveal a hint of unfet-tered cleavage. It was fitted in a wide band around her waist and then fell to the floor, hugging the lines of her body and flaring in a slight fishtail at the hem.

The material shimmered with a pearl-like lustre and moved with her body. He wanted to reach out and touch it so badly he knew he wouldn't be able to think of anything else all evening. How the silk would feel gliding against his hand, how her erect nipples would feel beneath the material, the warmth of the fabric beneath his touch, the give of her curves.

She wore a chunky three-strand choker of black pearls at her neck and he curled his hands into fists to stop himself from stroking them.

Maggie's heart gave a wild gallop at his appreciative gaze. 'Wow, yourself,' she murmured.

He looked like a model. It was the first time she'd seen him in anything remotely formal and the effect was mesmerising. His black tux was stunning and she couldn't decide which Nash was more handsome—the Levi's Nash or the tuxedo Nash. Her brain flashed another image on her inward eye and she gave herself a mental slap.

Naked Nash, of course.

Nash's gaze roved over her face, memorising every detail. She'd done her eyes up tonight with dark kohl and heavy mascara and they looked sultry and seductive. Luring him, tempting him to pick her up and spend all night here, in bed. Then he noticed the artful application of make-up on her temple and he pulled his mind out of his pants.

'How are you feeling?' he asked, lifting his hand to stroke her fringe back, inspecting the site closely.

Maggie pulled away from his touch. She rolled her eyes. 'I'm fine.'

'Are you sure?' he pressed.

Maggie knew if they didn't leave right now she was going to burst into tears. She couldn't take his concern. Not when it was motivated out of friendship and some sense of honour or guilt. He looked dashing and sexy tonight and she wanted nothing more than to drag him inside by his lapels and forget the damn ball.

But she was in an emotionally precarious state. The last thing she wanted to do was blurt out how she felt about him—all that would do was complicate things even further.

'Yes, Nash.' She moved forward, forcing him to step back, shutting the door behind her. She brushed past him and headed for his car.

Nash turned and watched her progress. The dress was totally backless and he almost groaned aloud.

How was he supposed to keep his hands off that?

The music coming from the band on the stage pulsed around the darkened ballroom and

Maggie watched with envy as a crowd of party-goers, including Nash, let their hair down on the dance floor. The tables were decorated with floating red candles, silver tinsel, red linen serviettes and lush green holly. The flames flickered and twinkled in the array of wineglasses cluttering the table and shimmered in the tinsel.

There was plenty to keep her mind off the dance floor, however. She'd reached minor celebrity status, being inundated in the early part of the evening by colleagues coming up to ask how she was and chat about the incident of the previous night. It had obviously rocketed around the grapevine and while she appreciated people's concern, between them and Nash she was about ready to scream.

Her gaze flicked back to the dancers. Nash was up there with Zoe from A and E. If it was at all possible he looked even sexier than he had when he'd been standing on her doorstep, which only increased her bad mood.

He'd wasted no time in modifying the tux,

undoing the jacket buttons so the lapels gaped as he boogied exposing an expanse of chest clad in a classic white shirt. He'd untied the bow-tie so it hung casually down from the confines of the collar. The top two buttons of his shirt had been relieved of their duty.

With his hair all mussed from dancing, he looked like a movie star at an Oscars after-party. And he'd been wildly popular despite his initial reluctance to leave her side. But she'd bitten down hard on her jealousy and urged him to go and dance. Anything to get some relief from his polite attentiveness and his damn aftershave.

She'd thought it would help. But it hadn't. She was miserable. It was some weird kind of self-inflicted torture, forcing herself to watch him with a string of other women. To face the reality of her life. Oh, sure, she knew there was nothing sexual about it, that Nash was just being a gentleman. But the truth was that he was going to London and there were going to be other women. She might as well get used to it.

The song came to an end and Nash returned to the table and threw himself into the seat beside her. He'd much rather be dancing with Maggie but the lure of her bare back and fudge-brownie eyes were lethal and at least on the dance floor he was removed from the temptation.

'Boy, it's hot out there,' he said, taking a swig of his frosty beer. 'How are you? Okay? Is your head aching?'

Maggie sighed. 'I'm fine, Nash.'

'Are you tired? We can leave any time.'

Maggie glared at him now, tired of being treated like a fragile piece of blown glass. 'I swear to God, Nash, if you ask me one more time, I'm going to pour that beer over your head.'

Nash chuckled and held up his hands in surrender. 'Okay, okay.'

A woman Maggie recognised from X-ray tapped Nash on the shoulder and he smiled at her. Maggie wanted to scratch her eyes out.

Nash stood to go with her but took a moment to bend down so his mouth was close to

Maggie's ear. 'We're leaving soon whether you like it or not.'

Maggie tracked his progress through the people milling around the edge of the dance floor, guiding his partner through the crush like a true gentleman, enjoying the back view as much as the front. How had she ever let herself fall in love with him? Her chest felt tight and her head gave a throb.

'So. You and Nash, huh?'

Maggie turned to Linda, who'd finally returned from the dance floor after what seemed like hours.

'Yes. Me and Nash.' She hoped she didn't sound as depressed as she felt.

'You kept that quiet.'

Maggie shrugged. 'It wasn't anything, really. Just a fling.'

'Friends with privileges?'

Maggie nodded, looking down at the starched white tablecloth. 'Something like that.'

'Except…'

'Yes. Except.' Their fling had borne some pretty serious consequences.

'Is he still going to London?'

'Yep.'

'Do you love him?'

Maggie looked up at her friend. 'Yep.' What was the point in hiding it?

'Oh, Maggie.'

Linda gave her shoulder a squeeze and Maggie shrugged it off. She could hear the pity in her friend's voice. Even Linda knew the folly of falling for Nash. 'It's okay.'

'C'mon,' Phil said, tugging on his wife's hand. 'There's still another hour to go before the band finishes.'

'Are you going to be okay?' Linda asked, resisting the pull.

'Of course. Go. Don't be silly.' Maggie plastered a smile on her face. 'Go!' she insisted again when Linda seemed hesitant.

Ten minutes later, Maggie was yawning as a sudden wave of exhaustion crept over her. She hated to admit that Nash was right but maybe the best place for her was home in bed. The band struck up a familiar tune and Maggie felt an awareness surround her like an aura.

Two hands slid down her bare shoulders from behind and a raging inferno spread through her veins like quicksilver. Nash leaned down, his lips close to her ear. 'They're playing our song, "Maggie May." Dance with me then I'll take you home.'

'Thought no dancing was part of the deal.'

'I'm making an exception.'

Maggie was too everything to resist. Too tired. Too needy. Too in love. She just turned and he pulled her chair out and helped her to her feet.

The band started to sing as he twirled her onto the dance floor. He held her close but not too close, aware of the speculation on the faces of their fellow dancers. Their secret was well and truly out and he'd fielded quite a few questions over the course of the evening, but it was important to him as he held her that everyone realised Maggie was more than just a conquest to him.

He slid his hand to the centre of her bare back,

resisting the urge to slide it down to her cute derrière and pull her hips closer. She swayed against him to the music, his body tightening everywhere, the movement and the bare skin of her back erotic beyond words.

There was a strange constriction in his chest as her perfume, her essence washed over him. Something shifted inside him, trampled by a surge of feelings that couldn't be contained.

'Have I told you you look beautiful tonight?' he murmured, looking down into her face as the blinking, colourful lights from the stage played across her cheekbones. Her eyelashes, thick and luscious with mascara, drew him in deeper, closer. There was a swelling in his chest that was growing by the second.

Maggie could barely breathe at the intensity of his gaze. It was making her dizzy. 'You scrub up pretty good for a country bumpkin yourself.'

He grinned at her. 'I feel like an undertaker.'

She shook her head. 'You look like a movie star.'

Nash tightened his hand against her back as his

chest filled to bursting with an emotion that was scaring the life out of him. 'So do you.' And then he dipped her quickly because he didn't know what was happening.

Maggie gave a startled cry and grabbed hold of his shoulders. When he hoisted her back to her feet it hit him like the proverbial tonne of bricks.

He loved her. He was in love with Maggie Green. The mother of his child.

Nash dropped all pretence of distance and pulled her closer as he processed the realisation that had come out of left field. She didn't protest, just laid her cheek against his chest, and he felt his stomach flutter. Like teenagers!

How had he been so blind?

Especially now he could pinpoint the exact moment he'd fallen for her. At the cafeteria that day, the first day he'd met her. She'd knocked him back and from that moment he'd been hooked. But it hadn't been until yesterday, seeing her lying in that pool of blood, facing those few awful seconds when he'd thought she was dead, that he'd been shaken out of his comfortable existence enough to start examining things.

He'd stupidly mistaken love for his ingrained sense of duty and honour. Telling himself instead that she was his responsibility. She and the baby were his duty. But holding her close like this now, feeling her body move against his, knowing their baby was nestled between them, he knew he'd made a grave error. He knew he loved her more than he'd ever loved anything in his life.

But did she feel the same way? She'd never indicated she had deeper feelings for him and had seemed more than fine with him going overseas and being a remote father for the first couple of years. She hadn't clung to him like more than one woman from his past had done, she hadn't asked him to stay or had a tantrum that he was leaving.

Maybe she'd got the one thing from him that she'd always wanted—a baby—and he was totally superfluous to her. A third wheel. Excess baggage. Collateral damage. Even thinking about it made him feel panicked and desperate. She had to love him back. She just had to.

He didn't want to be an outsider in his family. Live across the other side of the world while the woman he loved built a relationship with his child without him. While they became a family without him. He wanted to be a part of the family.

He knew then and there that he couldn't go to London. Didn't want to go. And, surprisingly, it didn't even matter. Only Maggie mattered. Maggie and his baby.

Maggie almost sighed as the warm cotton of his shirt caressed her cheek and one beautifully rounded pectoral formed a perfect pillow. She was weary and it was stuffy on the dance floor, crammed full of hot, sweaty bodies.

Nash's heartbeat thudded in her ear and she shut her eyes, letting its rhythm and the drift of starch and his aftershave lull her into a world where just the two of them existed. She felt light-headed as the crush around them loomed close and she leant into him a little more.

'Let's get out of here,' Nash said as the song drew to an end. He wanted to get her home and talk to her.

Maggie pulled her head off his chest and felt the room shift.

'Whoa. Maggie?' Nash grabbed her as she swayed away from him. 'What's wrong?' he demanded, his pulse rate skyrocketing as images of her still, bloodied body returned to taunt him. Was something going on in her head? Damn it, he should have insisted she have the X-ray.

'Nothing,' Maggie said faintly, pushing against the imprisoning wall of his chest. 'It's just so hot in here.'

Nash didn't like the look of her sudden pallor and swept her up into his arms.

'Nash!' she protested, clinging to his neck weakly, watching the jaws of bystanders drop as he strode out of the ballroom.

'We're leaving. Don't argue.'

* * *

Maggie daren't talk in the car on the way back to her place. Nash's face, usually so laid-back and relaxed, was as dark as thunder. She knew he was blaming himself for their early departure and really didn't want to hear an I-told-you-so from him.

He turned the engine off outside her place and she opened her mouth to speak to tell him it had just been a bit of light-headedness.

Nash let the buckle of the seat belt clink against the window as he threw it off his shoulder. 'Don't,' he growled.

Maggie sat while he strode around to her side, opened the door, helped her out and kept a firm grip on her as they walked up the path. 'I'm—'

'Don't,' he repeated.

Maggie waited while he opened her door and followed him into the lounge room. She'd left the Christmas tree lights on but even they failed to elevate his mood.

'Sit.' Nash pointed to the lounge chair.

Maggie was tempted to say *Yes, master* but

thought it wise not to push. He paced for a bit and she watched without comment. He stopped and looked down at her then resumed his pacing, shrugging out of his jacket and flinging it on the coffee table.

She found herself hoping he wouldn't stop there. There was something about brooding, intense Nash that was darkly sexy.

'I'm not going to London.'

Maggie blinked, dragging her mind out of the gutter. *So not what she'd expected him to say.* She'd expected a lecture about the stupidity of going out after a concussion. That he'd warned her it was folly. Of thinking about her health and the baby. All things loaded with duty and re- sponsibility. 'Wh what?'

'You heard me.'

He looked foreboding but she stood anyway. 'What are you talking about?'

Nash pointed to the chair. 'Sit.'

Maggie raised an eyebrow at him. 'Nash, for goodness' sake—I was a bit dizzy. That's all.

Please refrain from talking to me like I'm a dog.'

Nash shut his eyes briefly and pushed a hand through his hair. 'Sorry. I'm sorry, Maggie. It's just that…' He stopped. How could she know what that dreadful, gut wrenching moment had been like when he'd rounded that corner? 'I thought you were dead last night. I thought he'd killed you. For a moment. The blood was… And you looked so pale just now. Like last night.' He faltered. 'I just felt ill.'

Maggie frowned. He was talking like someone who really cared. Well, she supposed he did. She was his lover, the mother of his child. But his concern seemed to transcend the boundaries of duty. 'So what are you saying? You look at me and feel guilty and because of that you're not going to London?'

'Yes. No.' Nash clenched his fists. Yes, he did feel guilt, he should have been there. But it wasn't why he was staying. 'I'm not explaining this very well.'

'So explain it better.'

Nash took a deep breath. 'Dancing with you tonight, I had a sudden realisation. It's never happened to me before, which is possibly why I didn't recognise it ages ago when it first hit me between the eyes. I mean, I honestly didn't think it ever would because it just wasn't my aim. I have my career and my promise to my sister and that just takes priority.'

Maggie looked at him even more confused now. 'So…?'

Nash sighed. He was making a total hash out of it. 'I love you, Maggie. I'm in love with you.'

Maggie stared at him for a moment before groping for the chair behind her and sinking into it. He wouldn't joke about something like this, would he? Maybe he was confusing his fear for her and the baby last night with something else.

Nash rushed forward, kneeling before her. She'd gone pale again. Maybe he shouldn't have dropped this kind of bombshell in her delicate state. 'Are you okay? I think we should go back to the hospital.'

Maggie ignored him. 'Nash, I understand that I gave you a fright yesterday but you really don't need to make any rash declarations.'

Oh, God, she didn't love him back. An incredible bleakness swept through him as he contemplated life loving a woman who didn't return his feelings. Even with his love beating a tattoo in his chest, the knowledge was devastating.

He took her hands. 'There's nothing rash about it. I think I've known since the day I met you, I just didn't have any past experience to help me analyse it. I love you. And the baby. I want us to be a family. Together. Here. Not from the opposite side of the world. I'm just sorry it took me so long to get it.'

Maggie looked into his eyes and started to hope. He looked utterly sincere. His face solemn, his tropical-island eyes serious. There was no sign of laid-back Nash. In fact, he looked in pain, like he couldn't bear the swell of feelings inside him.

And she knew he was telling the truth.

'I know that you may not feel the same way and that—'

Maggie cut him off with her mouth, pressing a hard kiss against his unsuspecting lips. 'Oh, Nash,' she whispered as tears welled in her eyes. 'Stupid man. Of course I feel the same way.'

She gave him a watery smile. 'I know I wasn't supposed to fall for you. I know we had an understanding. And I know that I went and mucked that up by falling pregnant. And I know that I'm older than you. But I'm sorry, I did anyway. I just went and fell for you anyway.'

Nash let her words sink in for a moment, settling around the lump of dread that had started to rise from the pit of his stomach. Pushing it down, dissolving it like a snowman in sunlight. 'Really?'

Maggie nodded. 'Really.'

Nash suddenly felt lighter than air. He grinned at her. Then he stood, dragging her up with him, lifting her in his arms and twirling her round and round. Maggie laughed and held on tight.

He finally placed her on the floor. 'Are you sure, Maggie?'

She nodded. 'But what about you? You're the one who's going to be lumbered with an older woman.'

Nash's head swooped down for a deeply passionate kiss. 'I love you, Maggie. For the first time in my life I've fallen in love with an incredible woman. Last night you were on the floor in a pool of blood and I thought I'd lost you. Age is so irrelevant compared to that.'

Maggie stood on tiptoes and kissed him. He was right. If last night had taught them anything it was that life was short and was there to be lived. They didn't talk for a long time then. Their kisses got deeper and eventually they tumbled back onto the lounge behind them.

Maggie put a finger against his mouth as Nash homed in on her lips. 'Wait a moment.'

'I'm sorry.' He smiled, kissing her finger. He took a breath, desperately trying to dampen the fiery furnace burning in his belly. 'We shouldn't be doing this. You must be exhausted.'

She traced his jaw line with her finger. 'No. I meant we can do this any time. Let's get the really important thing out of the way. Let's go and book me an air fare.'

Nash frowned. 'What?'

'I'm going to London with you.'

The furrows in his brow got deeper. 'It's okay, Maggie. I don't have to go to London. I can complete my training here in Australia. I know you don't want to go and nothing is more important to me than you.'

Maggie smiled, her heart filling with love. She pushed against his chest and they both struggled into a sitting position. 'Not even the promise you made to yourself after your sister died? Great Ormond Street's the best, Nash. The best.'

'Yesterday it was the best. Today it's just another hospital on the other side of the world, keeping me away from you.' He slid his hand to her stomach. 'From the baby.'

She rested her head against his chest as his words swelled in her head and a lump of pure emotion expanded her chest to an unbearable tightness. He really did love her. He was reforging his set-in-stone career path for her. 'It won't be on the other side of the world if we're there with you.'

'Maggie,' Nash said, placing a finger under her chin and lifting it so he could see straight into her eyes. 'It's not important. I know you don't want to go.'

She smiled at him, cupping his face in her hands. 'I do. I do if you love me. If you want to commit, if you want to be a family with me and the baby, I'll follow you anywhere, Nash. I just didn't want to go on some whim to appease your sense of honour and responsibility. I didn't want to travel to the other side of the world just to see how it panned out. But, Nash, you loving me makes all the difference.'

Nash's heart beat painfully in his chest, fighting for room past the constriction in his throat. 'Really?'

She nodded. 'Of course. Wherever you are, that's where I want to be.'

'Even in the middle of the outback where the nearest supermarket or movie theatre is hundreds of kilometres away?'

'Especially there,' she whispered.

Nash shut his eyes and placed a hand over hers. He opened them again and looked into her eyes again. The tree lights danced in her irises. 'What did I do to deserve you?'

'Something good, I think.'

Nash smiled. 'Looks like Santa came early,' he murmured against her mouth.

Maggie gave a soft laugh, their lips touching. 'It's going to be Christmas all year from now on.'

Nash chuckled. 'Ho, ho, ho.'

EPILOGUE

MAGGIE MANAGED TO convince Nash the next morning she was perfectly capable of going into work for her shift. They drove to his place so he could change his clothes and then headed into work full of Christmas spirit, despite not getting much sleep.

And she was pleased she did. They were able to give Alice and Brett the best Christmas gift they were ever going to get—they extubated Toby. With the tube out, Toby's silent cries finally had a voice, if a little croaky.

He was even able to get out of bed and have a proper cuddle with his parents. Best of all, for the first time in weeks, safely snuggled in his mother's arms, he gave them all a great big smile.

'This is just the best,' Alice said, looking down at a happy Toby with tears in her eyes. 'There were a couple of times I thought this day would never come.'

Nash and Maggie exchanged looks. Toby's parents hadn't been alone in their pessimistic view.

After lunch Nash sidled up to Maggie. 'Thanks for my gift,' he murmured, rubbing the gum nuts together. 'Guess we'll both be able to keep in touch with our roots while we're over there.'

Maggie nodded, the smell of eucalyptus wafting towards her. 'Guess so.'

'You missed your Secret Santa gift,' he said.

She frowned. 'No, I didn't. I opened it while you were on round. I got a coffee mug.'

Nash raised an eyebrow. 'Really? But I just saw one under the tree for you.'

Maggie looked puzzled as she walked towards the tree. 'I must have missed it. It's probably part of the first gift. They must have become separated,' she mused as she bent to retrieve the small package wrapped in a red ribbon.

'Hmmm,' Nash said noncommittally, grinning like an idiot behind her.

Maggie opened the second gift without giving it a lot of thought, pretty sure it'd probably be some kind of accessory to the first. Maybe a box of tea bags or something.

It wasn't until she hit blue velvet that she realised the gift wasn't from her Secret Santa. But from Nash. She turned to face him, her hands shaking.

'Nash?'

Nash smiled down at her. 'Open it,' he murmured.

Maggie's fingers were trembling so badly it seemed to take an age to prise the lid open. When she finally managed it, the ring took her breath away. A large square cut blue sapphire sat on the plump velvet cushion.

'Oh, Nash,' she whispered, unable to tear her gaze away from it.

Nash, his own fingers a little on the trembly side, took it out of the box. He'd made such a hash of the last proposal he was determined to make this one special.

'Will you make me the happiest man in the world, Maggie? Will you marry me?'

Maggie couldn't believe it. The background noise of the unit faded as the world narrowed down to just the two of them at this moment.

In a few short months all her dreams had come true. She, the man she loved and their baby were going to become a family. 'Yes.' She smiled, looking into his incredible blue eyes.

Applause rang out around the unit as they became aware of their surroundings again. Nash grinned at her as he placed the ring on her finger. 'Merry Christmas, Maggie May.'

Maggie stood on tiptoe and wound her arms around his neck. 'This is going to be a hard Christmas to top.'

'I'm going to spend the rest of my life doing just that,' he promised.

And they kissed in front of a very appreciative audience.

MEDICAL™

Large Print

Titles for the next three months...

June

SNOWBOUND: MIRACLE MARRIAGE	Sarah Morgan
CHRISTMAS EVE: DOORSTEP DELIVERY	Sarah Morgan
HOT-SHOT DOC, CHRISTMAS BRIDE	Joanna Neil
CHRISTMAS AT RIVERCUT MANOR	Gill Sanderson
FALLING FOR THE PLAYBOY MILLIONAIRE	Kate Hardy
THE SURGEON'S NEW-YEAR WEDDING WISH	Laura Iding

July

POSH DOC, SOCIETY WEDDING	Joanna Neil
THE DOCTOR'S REBEL KNIGHT	Melanie Milburne
A MOTHER FOR THE ITALIAN'S TWINS	Margaret McDonagh
THEIR BABY SURPRISE	Jennifer Taylor
NEW BOSS, NEW-YEAR BRIDE	Lucy Clark
GREEK DOCTOR CLAIMS HIS BRIDE	Margaret Barker

August

EMERGENCY: PARENTS NEEDED	Jessica Matthews
A BABY TO CARE FOR	Lucy Clark
PLAYBOY SURGEON, TOP-NOTCH DAD	Janice Lynn
ONE SUMMER IN SANTA FE	Molly Evans
ONE TINY MIRACLE...	Carol Marinelli
MIDWIFE IN A MILLION	Fiona McArthur

MILLS & BOON®